# SCENES FROM A CLINICAL LIFE

# SCENES FROM A CLINICAL LIFE
## A Novel

*R. L. Jannaway*

**KARNAC**

First published in 2016 by
Karnac Books Ltd
118 Finchley Road
London NW3 5HT

British Library Cataloguing in Publication Data

A C.I.P. for this book is available from the British Library

ISBN-13: 978-1-78220-443-5

Typeset by Medlar Publishing Solutions Pvt Ltd, India

Printed in Great Britain by TJ International Ltd, Padstow, Cornwall

www.karnacbooks.com

# ONE

It was a day at the end of summer. The light seemed to shimmer with a piercing clarity. The elderberries were turning from green to gleaming black, and the sloes were beginning to look like dusty blue globes in the hedgerows. David Treuherz was partly aware of the incandescent light but was more concerned with getting his car started, and himself to the interview. The car was a make that he had imagined would not only convey his person but would also project an image of him as rather alternative and unusual. He was relieved when it started; it was a cheap car, with an idiosyncratic tendency to inexplicable inertness, and he knew that sooner or later he would have to get it attended to.

Successfully on his way, he headed out to the suburb where he was being interviewed for a job as a clinical psychologist in a child and adolescent mental health consultation service. It would be his first job since qualifying as a child psychologist, though he worked privately with adults as a psychodynamic counsellor. He glanced anxiously at himself in the mirror as he drove, checking his tie. His hazel-coloured eyes looked back at him nervously, and he had to make an effort to be calm, smoothing back the black tuft of hair that flopped on to his forehead. He ran through the answers to questions he might be asked, half his attention on the driving and the increasing greenery as he approached the suburb. A jay flew across the road almost under his wheels and he delighted at seeing so clearly the warmth of its colouring in the brilliant light, feeling that it was a good omen.

The clinic was housed in a large modern building. On three floors, it was surrounded by grassed gardens, and a fine holly tree in front was covered in small waxy scarlet berries. He was impressed by the pleasant environment as he was invited through from the waiting room to the interview.

He got the job. He was not to know in this first meeting what he later discovered—that the interdisciplinary discussions between the members of the clinical team were ongoing. Discussions went on over the right way to deal with the animal residents of the building, the cats that inhabited the warm corners of the house; over clinical issues; over the way the service was managed: in fact, over every issue. He would be enlivened by the discussions, inevitably. The group of longstanding experienced members of the team was made up of staff who had qualified long since and were steady and resourceful. The psychiatrist held the dominant position in this group. The child psychotherapist, Ann, who belonged to this group, was preoccupied during his first weeks in the job, coming to him later and apologising for not linking in with him more actively. She confessed to some personal issues to do with a difficult relationship, which was breaking down … this was frank, and he thought the more of her for her honesty. Her position in the longstanding experienced group meant that she had a lot to offer him. The new group of young clinicians, of which he was part, was led by the principal clinical psychologist whom he had been impressed by at his interview. It was the discussions between her and the child psychiatrist that underlay the lively atmosphere of the team.

Discussion was constant. No opportunity was lost by the child psychiatrist to make lively comments at odd moments during the working day. The psychiatrist was a skilled clinician, and challenged thinking amongst the team members. David was glad of the unobtrusive support of his clinical psychologist senior, who kept herself to herself and generally worked hard in a concentrated way, but was highly regarded and sought for consultation by both groups of staff, old and new. And, in fact, David found that concentrating on the work, modelling his work persona on hers, served not only to give the *impression* that the work was going well, but that in reality it *was* going well. He was fortunate in that he found the work involving and rewarding. In his engagement with the troubled families who came to the clinic, referred by their family doctors, there was a ready focus for his days. He found another experienced clinician outside the work setting who could offer him an extra weekly space to think through his clinical encounters, and he found this invaluable. It also served to buffer him from the stress of working routinely with a population of families for whom difficulties were entrenched and where long-term work was likely to be necessary.

It was fortunate for David that an old friend was also starting work in a new job at the same time. He and Jack Threlfall had been friends since encountering each other on their first day at secondary school. They had found that their common inter-ests meant that they had often sat in the same classes together, played music in the same groups, and were in the same sports teams. Shortly after they had both started in their new work settings they met for supper in a café adjacent to the park. It was a dark little place with Viennese pastries in the chiller cabinet, dusty oil paintings of Dutch landscapes on the walls, and tables set outside under umbrellas on the quiet tree-lined road so that patrons could enjoy the sunshine.

They compared notes. Their paths had diverged slightly; David had moved on from school to a degree followed by studies in psychodynamic counselling and clinical psychology—the counselling studied at a fringe and small, rather alternative counselling organisation; whereas Jack, from a medical family, had allowed the inherited genes to prompt him in the direction of medicine. Jack was now pursuing his studies in psychotherapy, having qualified as a psychiatrist, working at the prestigious Limes clinic in a full-time clinical post, which helped him with his training at the same time.

Both felt a little overwhelmed in their new posts. Jack had organisational pressure to contend with, but rather more challenging was the anxiety engendered in him by his working at such an august institution, with its worldwide reputation, its pinnacled Edwardian architecture, and its boundlessly erudite senior members of staff who had often trained as psychotherapists at the Radcliffe. This was an organisation that had long held its position amongst the more well-known of the psychotherapy organisations with ease, bolstered up by the pro-psychoanalytic zeitgeist of the last half of the twentieth century, and the ready supply of people who wanted to train as psychotherapists, or to have supervision for their psychotherapy work.

There was a lot to mull over together as they lingered over their Mittel-European dinners, unaware that the place they had chosen for their meal echoed their interest in psychoanalytic thinking, the Viennoiserie of the little café echoing the Viennese antecedents of the psychotherapy world they were both moving into. They were glad of the opportunity to talk

4

over their daily struggles, and the habitual ease of their conversation, based as it was on such a long friendship, was a comfort to both.

"I'm going to a conference soon," David said, with half a thought that Jack might be interested. Jack stopped with a fork filled with chestnut and chocolate torte half way to his mouth. He put his fork down, leant back in his chair, and ran his hand through his ruffled golden hair. Stockily built, his blue eyes gleaming behind his fashionable glasses, he gave David a lively harangue on the difficulties of taking any time away from his heavy schedule of clinical work, study, and the personal training therapy that his course demanded.

"What's it about, anyway?" he asked, polishing his glasses on his napkin with a characteristically lively flourish.

"It's called 'Child and family consultation services: organisational difficulties endemic?', with, I suspect, the emphasis on group dynamics—the man running it's a group analyst," said David. They both laughed at the apposite title, and Jack said that he was too busy to go, despite the interesting subject.

"Oh well—it'll give me a break from Feline Manor," David said.

"Feline Manor? Meaning?" Jack glanced at his plate, clearly regretting the fact that it was all but empty.

"Haven't I told you about the resident cats at work?" David replied. "The wonderful cats loitering about when you go into the building? There's even a sleek tom that sits on the stairs. Bats at unsuspecting people with its paw through the banisters."

"I hope he keeps his claws in," said Jack. "Not very welcoming for the families coming to the service."

"I suppose not. Though some of the children seem to quite like it," said David.

Jack immediately topped this story with his own about his workplace. Many young clinicians were trained there … but could any of them be persuaded to a sociable smile, when picking up their patients from the waiting room? He himself would be nervous of this quiet person taking him to a room bare except for a chair, tables, and probably, for children, a box of toys … David laughed and said (in pontificatory mode) that maybe he didn't know yet that it was important not to seduce the patient with too much niceness, or to spoil the developing *transference*.

"Transference? You mean the feelings the patient develops towards the therapist? The ones that more properly belong to early family relationships?" David smiled at Jack's ironic tone and they were off into more talk about their respective work settings.

As David drove home after his dinner with Jack, he allowed himself a moment of envy as he considered their developing careers. His was moving actively towards working privately as a counsellor, while also remaining in the public sector "gulag". He was surprised with his choice of word, and then remarked to himself that there was indeed something almost Stalinist about the pressure of the need to work with as heavy a caseload as possible, and to do brief work so as to move the families through assessment and treatment quickly, with the minimum number of appointments. Underfunding was chronic, there weren't enough clinicians, and there was the constant pressure of a long waiting list. Jack's career, of course, was encompassed by the same public sector pressures, but he was working in a place that was a natural jumping-off point for training at the Radcliffe in due course. David, too, aspired to this training and to becoming a psychotherapist, but he was experienced enough to know that a medically trained person stood a greater chance of being accepted for a sought-after training than someone like himself with an arts degree and two clinical trainings, one at a rather alternative counselling organisation.

Arriving home, he put that thought out of his mind, only to have it replaced by memories of his recently ended relationship with a woman who had decided that travel to Brazil was preferable to what she termed, slightly contemptuously, as graft in the public sector. Sometimes, chiefly on Monday mornings, he was tempted to agree with her, but his career did have an excitement to it ... or was it, he remarked to himself, just a snare and a delusion? The psychotherapy world was full of people idealising the work in a masochistic way, and also idealising their trainings, their teachers, with the Radcliffe at the very summit of what was desirable. He laughed to himself. Would that make Jack the man who conquered Everest, while he might be destined to remain at base camp? He shook the thoughts off, both of Jack and his likely professional success, and his recent girlfriend's departure, and settled himself to preparing for the next day, with the warmth of the September sun still permeating the atmosphere in his flat and highlighting the faint scent of the freesias that his girlfriend had left in a vase on the mantelpiece.

A few weeks later David found himself—without Jack—assembling with others for the conference. It was held in a smart inner-city house with a double reception room sufficiently large to accommodate the group of about twenty. Through the window Jack could see a large apple tree, branches bowed with ripening apples. Thoughts emerged from the back of his mind about the time of year, along with the quotations that always came to him, this time centred on phrases from Keats' autumnal poem ... and he wondered if the climate must have been slightly warmer in Keats' time to have grape vines loaded and blessed with fruit. He found that his immediate neighbour in the chairs set out in a circle was a woman of about his age, pleasantly dressed in a skirt and matching blouse, legs bare and brown from the summer. Her green eyes caught his glance and she smiled, pushing back the straight, brown, shoulder-length hair, introducing herself as Clara. She said she too was a clinical psychologist, working partly in adult mental health and partly in child and family settings. And, she added, half-laughing at her audacity and self-promotion, "I'm just writing a book." He was about to push aside the competitiveness that, as usual, began its insidious work in the back of his mind, in order to ask her more about it, when the conference began.

Suffice it to say that the conference followed the usual pattern. They were invited to introduce themselves. The convenor gave a competent summary of the difficulties of organisational dynamics in child and family mental health settings. He gave his view that the difficulties were underpinned by the fact that three different funding streams supported the services—from health, education, and children's social care. They were invited to split into small groups and to discuss. Feedback to the larger group. Lunch.

Over lunch, David could see his new acquaintance talking warmly with someone on the far side of the room, laughing, pinning her hair back with one hand while she started the complicated business of tackling her plate of food at the same time as remaining standing. David moved purposefully in her direction, but his way was blocked by the child psychotherapist from his service who had cold-shouldered him initially. Ann was thin, with frizzy blond hair and earnest brown eyes behind gold-framed glasses. She began a conversation with him about the clinical capacity and experience (she thought impressive) of the newly appointed educational psychologists in their service for clinical work with families. By the time he had managed to extricate himself, with some difficulty but with a determination on politeness, from this entanglement, he found that Clara had disappeared and it wasn't until the lunch break was nearly over that he located her again in the kitchen.

As they sat down again he asked her whether she would like to go on somewhere at the end of the conference. She looked slightly nervous and declined, pleading the illness of her grandmother—or was it her mother?—and a promised hospital visit. Slightly resentfully he wondered to himself if he was so much the big bad wolf that she had to adopt a little Red Riding Hood persona and flee … then he laughed to himself at his fanciful idea, and they were again into discussion about organisational dynamics. At the end he did at least acquire her email address and phone number and had to be satisfied with that. He wasn't sure if her ring-free hand signified availability but philosophically said to himself that he would email. Less threatening for the slightly anxious, he assured himself.

# TWO

It was two weeks later that David was able to induce Clara to meet him for supper at the same café where he had met Jack. He could not ascertain from her manner and the relative freedom with which she had arranged to meet him whether she was in fact already in a relationship with someone else. He felt nervous as he waited for her, and she was clearly nervous too. She let the two sides of her hair hang down in front of her face, obscuring his view of her, until she began to relax and flicked one side up behind her ear. By the time they were on their dessert (chocolate and chestnut torte this time for him, with associated memories of his Swiss childhood; fruit salad for her) some of their mutual nervousness had declined. Each had discovered that the other was single. And David had discovered more about her book than his competitiveness would allow him easily to know. It was about childhood autism and psychological approaches to it.

His competitiveness was piqued, too, by her professional aspirations. Not content with her psychology doctorate, she was starting the application process to the Radcliffe and was clearly in a state of rather dazzled idealisation in relation to the issue, and the possibility that she might train as a psychotherapist. He bore with her patiently while she gave a lengthy account of her first interview. Through this account he did find out more about her. Her parents (lived in Kent), her degree, her cat. With this last he winced for a moment. Oh God! Not more cats! But she convinced him that this cat was modest in habit, affectionate, and prone to greeting her with warmth on her return from work, alleviating, she said, the pain of the end of a recent long-term relationship. He resisted the temptation to see her description of the cat as representing something of her character, and was openly sympathetic to her recent loss whilst secretly pleased that there might be a future in their relation-ship. He told himself that he needed to play his cards carefully, liking Clara more the more he saw of her. She was dressed stylishly this evening with earrings whose little purple glass drops were arranged like bunches of grapes, and her green eyes were set off by the minute leaves that twined in a necklace that matched the grape earrings. She was alert, intelligent, and lively, but not intrusively so, and listened to him with attention and warmth when he talked.

He discovered that she lived near him, and it wasn't long after this encounter that he got a call from her one evening. Her cat had gone missing—could he help her find her? Smiling to him-self he walked round to her house.

"I've found her," she announced as she opened the door, voice tremulous. He couldn't but help admire the front door, Edwardian stained glass in-filling the panel in the front, which was painted a delicate shade of grey-green. The grey-green matched the paint around the windows and gave a trim, coher-ent look to the front of the house. The garden was full of white Japanese anemones, tall and graceful.

"Good! Where was she?"

"She seems to be stuck in the ash tree. I don't know what to do—she won't come when I call." Clara looked white and strained and he realised that she was very attached to the cat.

11

"You could leave some food out for her overnight, she's bound to find her way down if you leave her." Clara looked alarmed and tearful.

"No-no—that won't do—she's frightened of the bully boy tom that lives next door—in fact she probably ran into the tree to escape him. Couldn't you get her down for me?" "Me?" said David incredulously. "What about the fire brigade?"

"No-no—that wouldn't help—they couldn't get their ladder into the back garden. Please, you can see it's a big tree, but quite easy to climb." He looked at the tree. She was right; once he had got into the lower branches it would be an easy climb.

"Alright then, I'll have a go. Have you got a chair I can stand on to get onto that first branch?" While she went into the house to get the chair he studied the situation. The ash tree was a big one, trunk solid and grey, the graceful pinnate leaves rustling slightly in the breeze. It was a lovely tree, shading the large back garden.

"Come on down, puss," he called up hopefully, but the little tabby cat clung to her branch and affected to look in the other direction. He had read somewhere that cats didn't like direct eye contact, so he also looked away and repeated his call. No response.

"Here you are," said Clara, setting the chair down firmly into the ground, testing it to make sure it was stable. He took off his jacket.

"Don't worry," he said, "we'll get her down." He said this with more confidence than he felt, but he set himself to climb the tree, wedging each foot in turn in the crook of the branches. Soon he seemed to be isolated in a green and whispering world as the tree engulfed him, and he avoided looking down so that he wouldn't realise how high he was getting. Clara kindly kept up a barrage of comment to distract him, saying encouraging things and talking to the cat.

*There* was the cat. It was a matter of getting along the branch to her. She clearly wasn't going to approach him, despite his attempts to call her enticingly. He was annoyed with himself for not having thought of bringing a scrap of food up with him to encourage her.

He paused, standing on the branch she was crouched on, one hand holding the trunk of the tree, which was reassuringly firm to his grasp. He wondered how to approach her without frightening her into jumping—or frightening himself too much. He decided to sit on the branch, one leg each side, and inch himself forward, and he did this, talking to her quietly as he did so. The branch swayed alarmingly and he hoped it wouldn't break or that the swaying would make her fall. She was looking at him now that he was close to her, and her eyes seemed enormous. He wondered if she really was stuck or would indeed come down in her own good time, but she let out a soft mew as he got nearer to her and he thought that she did need his help.

He reached out a hand to her gently, letting her approach him a little of her own free will. Her tabby fur was shining in the green glow from the tree and she mewed again as he inched forward. He reached her, and balancing himself with one hand, resorted to holding her by the loose fur at the back of her neck. She allowed herself to be tucked inside his shirt, unresisting, and he was mightily relieved that she was so docile. One wrong move would have both of them crashing down to the ground through the branches. He edged back towards the bole of the tree, hardly breathing as his weight seemed to bend the branch. It was difficult to move with this little cat pressed against his rib cage.

"Come on then," he said, as much to encourage himself as her, and it wasn't long before he had managed little by little to regain ground level. He jumped down from the chair and handed the little cat to Clara.

"Oh, thank you so much David," she said. It was the first time she had used his name and he was pleased—glad that he had successfully managed this climb, which had left him breathless and trembling—and he told himself that this was the only reason his knees were weak as she impulsively kissed him on the cheek. Clara set the cat down on the ground and, purring, she immediately twined around her legs affectionately.

"Come in, and have a drink—it's the least I can offer you," she said. He went in to her little kitchen and the two of them watched the cat attack her bowl of cat food with gusto, glancing sideways at them the while.

He told her, laughing, of the poem in which Baudelaire described his cat—a male cat, large and strong, but whose gaze would invariably be fixed on the poet whenever he happened to glance at him. She told David of the story of the wayward television newsreader some years previously, who, maybe a little tipsy, had laughed loudly on air as he described firefighters rescuing a cat only to run over it as they drove away afterwards.

"I'm walking, so no risk there," he laughed. "Don't hesitate to ask me to help if she gets above herself like that again," he said as he left, with the vague thought in the air between the two of them that they might meet again.

The next day he went as usual to his session with his psychotherapist, Dr Smythe. He was in his late sixties, with a shock of white hair balancing a vigorous bushy beard above which steady eyes looked out on the world as from a cave. He had retired some years previously from an out-of-town psychiatric unit where he had held a position as psychiatrist and psychotherapist, and now only worked with private patients. David counted himself lucky to be in therapy with so experienced a clinician, not least because his breadth of experience was linked to what David felt was a proper clinical understanding, a capacity for tact, and considerable warmth of personality. There was a real regard for the patient, and David felt that he was in the presence of someone who had benefitted from struggling with his own internal difficulties. This was especially important for David, as he thought of himself as someone who had needed to do likewise.

Dr Smythe had listened attentively to David's description of his background. David had been brought up until the age of six in Switzerland, where his Swiss father, a gifted linguist, had worked as an interpreter and translator along with a small amount of teaching and lecturing. His mother was English, also a gifted linguist, who had met his father in the sixties when colour and life were returning after the grim post-war period. David was the oldest of the family, a first child after their parents had lost their first baby at a few days old to meningitis. He himself had been premature, spending some weeks in an incubator in hospital before being released to his parents' anxious arms. His birth was followed rapidly by two younger sisters, one after another, and, it seemed to him in retrospect, welcomed into the world in a less anxious way. No anxieties, no trauma there! Blonde haired, good humoured and healthy, the house was enlivened with their giggles and constant chat and activity. They were a natural pair, being close together in age.

David found himself initially idealised by both parents as the child to replace the boy they had lost, but then found his father increasingly withdrawn as he began to suffer the mood swings and early signs of the depression that led to his suicide when David was sixteen. His mother was a steady presence. When the family moved to England when he was six he understood, at some level, that she needed the company of her own parents and sisters, to make up for her husband's increasing unavailability. He was not aggressive, just unavailable, and liked to spend long periods lost in his books and translating work, more so when they moved to England. He was pleasant enough to his in-laws and the children, but emotionally absent.

David's mother was a lively woman, not given to introspection, who found her husband's dark moods difficult to tolerate, but nevertheless continued her own academic work and the work of bringing up the family with a cheerful stoicism. It was only later that David would realise what she suffered in lacking a companion in his father.

It was clear in the work of the therapy with Dr Smythe that David had not been unaffected by the family constellation. It had a significant impact on his inner world. The therapeutic work benefitted from the positive feelings David had for his therapist, based not only on his competence and warmth, but also on the positive experiences David brought with him from his relationship with his mother and a much-loved grandfather. He was inclined to feel positively towards older figures of authority. David felt safe enough in the therapy to speak about the difficulties he had encountered at university in moving away from the family, leaving his sisters still at home, forging what felt like a lonely path towards an adulthood that seemed insecurely founded. David could allow himself to understand the early origins of the depression that struck him in his second year away at university. His sense of alienation at finding the move from home so difficult, which had lingered, began to be ameliorated.

He discussed with Dr Smythe the question of applying to the Radcliffe to train himself as a psychotherapist. In the lack of surprise with which this subject was received he sensed that his therapist had expected him to move in this direction. There was a positive response, as far as he could determine, since it was put very much in terms of his obviously finding the therapy helpful if he would himself like to train in more depth to use psychoanalytic techniques like his therapist ... There was a discussion about the need to change to a different psychotherapist, a therapist who would see him through the training, an idea which David found painful. He wondered why Dr Smythe could not himself be a training therapist. The answer was unequivocal: Dr Smythe was too old, he could not take patients who were trainees … David would have to change.

As a preliminary to applying, David arranged to meet with a psychotherapist from the Radcliffe, who was guarded about the possibility of finding a training therapist and equally guarded about the possibility of training. David had a counselling training, and the training in clinical psychology, why was that not enough? Why did he want to add on another training? Did he realise how expensive it would be? And so on. David was startled by this less than enthusiastic response to his wish to train, but he set it on one side and began seriously to consider the question of finding a training therapist. He had been with Dr Smythe for two years, and it would be a wrench to find someone new; but it would have to be done. Then there was a sudden difficulty. He was sitting at home one evening when the phone rang. He answered. It was the voice of a woman he didn't know.

"Mr Treuherz?"

"Yes?"

"I'm sorry to tell you that Dr Smythe has had a stroke. He won't be able to work for some time." David was speechless, feeling hardly able to frame any words to respond. The voice at the other end of the phone, a warm voice, clearly picking up his distress said something with some humour.

"I'm sorry, I didn't hear that," said David.

"I said that he isn't dead, he's had a stroke," said his caller, with, he felt, possibly some concern for his obvious shock.

"Of course," he gathered himself together to reply. "Will he call me when he's able to start work again?"

"He'll write and let you know," said his caller and rang off.

Stunned, David sat down, looking, without seeing, at his surroundings. What should he do? Dr Smythe might be unavailable for months. This thought was still with him when he got a letter a few days later from Dr Smythe letting him know that he would not be able to work for at least three or four months and that David should go ahead with his search for a training therapist if this felt appropriate. It did feel appropriate, particularly so since David knew that if he could start psychotherapy with a training therapist he was far more likely to be accepted.

David was, however, thrown into what he felt was a state of mind very similar to that in which he had been during his depressed time at university, when he had struggled to do the work on the course, and he now found a similar dynamic reasserting itself. He was very low, especially at weekends, and it was a relief when Jack, in an effort to help, invited him to play football with him and a group of other friends. He came to pick David up from his flat. As they drove over to the football field a few miles away, he remarked to David that it might be that his depression was linked to his father's suicide. Might not his therapist's sudden disappearance stir up feelings about the similarly sudden loss of his father? David thought he was right. He remembered the shock of his father's death. It had indeed precipitated a depression, which David had struggled with, just as each member of the family around him had also struggled to deal with the awful event. Each morning at that time he had awoken in buoyant spirits, only to feel crushed, almost physically, by the awareness of his father's death hitting him again.

His father had been in the habit of swimming alone in the evenings on their family holidays, this time in Portugal. They had been warned of the strong currents around a particular headland, and this was where his father was found dead after he had not come home from his evening swim. It wasn't officially listed as a suicide, but David and the rest of the family did not need an official view to be clear in their minds that it was increasing despondency that had led David's father to swim in this lonely and dangerous place, with an inevitable outcome.

David was grateful to Jack for the thought, especially so since he then retrieved his capacity to think about the meaning of his sudden and catastrophic depression. He remembered that Dr Smythe had linked his despair after his father's death to the early despair of the infant he had once been, alone in hospital after his premature birth. The incubator had functioned as a lifesaver—but also inculcated in his infantile self a painful sadness, a desperate pining for maternal warmth rather than clinical coldness. He had read somewhere that clinicians were now suggesting that premature babies should be nursed nestled close to their mothers to keep them warm, and that, unsurprisingly, this had a better clinical outcome.

He had been musing silently on all this when he realised that they had arrived at the football field. Jack introduced him to those of the others he didn't know, a sprinkling of Limes clinicians and some psychotherapists. The field was surrounded by tall poplars, a pleasant green sunlit space. They had to create room for their ad hoc game by moving a group of small boys, also playing football, to further down the field. There were enough players to make a scratch game and the exercise began to lift David's mood. He found himself laughing immoderately as one less fit and less able player picked up a midfield pass, and in a display of ungainly effort somehow managed to keep the ball moving and bouncing backwards out of his uncoordinated control until he had scored an own goal.

David enjoyed the game, except for the behaviour of one of the players, a Russian psychotherapist called Georg, who kept barging him, pushing him when he had the ball—an over-extravagant style that almost had David barging him back.

A different style of playing, he said to himself, and, afterwards, in conversation with him, discovered a thick accent masking a warmth of personality sufficient for him to forgive him. Not, however, without wondering maliciously to himself how he could be a therapist when his English was so difficult to understand. He was a good-looking, rather trim man, black-haired like David. David had a moment of what he hoped was not prescient unease. Georg said he worked in the same adult psychotherapy unit as Clara. He did not like to imagine Clara in conversation with Georg. He knew already that she was prone to idealise the Radcliffe; might she not also feel similarly about therapists like Georg? Examining him, David decided that he was not good-looking enough to tempt such an attractive woman … however, his doubts were sufficient to have him telephoning Clara that evening, asking her out. She was busy. She was sorry. She let him know very gently (she was sympathetic to the sudden loss of his psychotherapist) that in fact she was very caught up with her mother's illness and could not go out during this latest difficulty.

They talked for a while on the phone. He asked her about her mother's illness and heard that it was serious, but that she would recover in time. She promised to call him. He was disappointed. He arranged to go out for a meal with another friend who listened attentively to the story of his failure to make progress in setting up a more secure relationship with Clara.

David was also disappointed in his efforts to find a training therapist. Ringing psychotherapists about vacancies he was often regretfully told that they needed to keep any possible vacancy for people who had already been accepted to train at the Radcliffe. They could not run the risk of taking him on for treatment, only to find that he was not accepted to train. He could see the logic of this but nevertheless he was downcast. He sought advice from Jack, who had been successful in finding a training therapist, no doubt because, having a medical qualification, he was quite likely to be accepted. With his usual quick mind and active approach Jack suggested that he ring a senior therapist involved in the training, and get help with the issue, so David did that. He explained to her that he had contacted at least ten psychotherapists in a bid to be taken on and she said that this could not be possible. Surprised at her not believing him he said that it was, indeed, possible, and that he had been assiduous in his efforts. She said that she would find him a psychotherapist, which cheered him a great deal, but his new positivity was undermined somewhat by the events at a party that same evening.

It was a launch party for a book that had been written by some family therapists along with some psychotherapists about psychoanalytic thinking in work with families and couples, and he had been invited to attend by the family therapist from his service who had made a contribution to the book. Arriving at the party, which was held at the Limes clinic, David found that he did not know many people. He moved to get a glass of wine and as he did so caught sight of Clara laughing enthusiastically at something someone was saying. His heart sank as he realised that it was Georg, the Russian therapist, who was so impressing her. She caught sight of him the same moment, waved merrily over Georg's shoulder, and continued what was clearly a fascinating conversation. Disconsolate, he found himself talking to a family therapist from his clinic. It was a relief when speeches were given and he could leave, not without noticing that Clara was walking in front of him down the corridor as he left, holding hands with Georg and talking animatedly. He tried to greet the sight with some equanimity, but it was difficult.

Back in his flat he sat at the window overlooking the garden and brooded quietly on the fact that he had not moved quickly enough with Clara. She obviously liked him—but liked Georg and the fact that he was at the Radcliffe more. He chided himself with having shown such obvious signs that he was interested in her. She must have been aware of his heightened colour when he took her out, his liveliness. Reflecting on all this he remembered suddenly that it was his mother's birthday. She lived not far from him in a Victorian terraced cottage and he rang, thinking of dropping in to see her. As usual, she was delighted to hear from him and he invited himself around to see her—she was going to go out with friends later and he just had time to call in. He gave her a card and some flowers. She was a tall woman, almost matching his lanky height, hair still luxuriant and dark, and a lively presence. He was momentarily returned to the fond feelings of childhood, picking up faint traces of her favourite perfume and make-up as he gave her a hug and kiss. She was clearly a little tired but seemed bright.

He began to tell her of his woes with Clara and the illness of his therapist. She was concerned about Clara, but, he noticed, less than sympathetic about his therapist's absence. "What do you need therapy for, David?" she asked, pursing her lips as she surveyed the arrangement of the flowers she had made in a vase. "You had that little difficulty at Oxford, but that's all over now. Surely you don't need any more help from these people?"

He found himself protesting. "It wasn't exactly a little difficulty," he said, remembering the depression that had overcome him.

"But that was a long time ago," she objected. "I can't understand why you need to pay all this money for psychotherapy now."

"We've been through this before," he said impatiently. He explained once again the necessity for psychotherapists in training to have their own therapy, not only to help them make

sense of their own internal worlds but also to help them understand their patients from the inside, as it were.

As the conversation proceeded along the lines it had taken
many times before he wondered how it was that such an
intelligent and sensitive person as his mother could not seem
to understand what he was saying. She taught German at a
university, and was in contact with many students—and
some of them must have difficulties, he protested to himself.
How was it that she could not see the need for people to have
help? He knew that she was not someone given to considering internal reality, despite her deep understanding of German
literature, but her intransigence on this point defeated him.
Was it that she didn't like the idea of her son needing help,
when her husband, his father, had clearly had so many difficulties? She might be worried that he would head down the same
road. He decided that this might be it.

He lightened the atmosphere between them deliberately.
   "Have you heard the one about the competitive mothers?"
he asked her. She sensed that she was about to be diverted
from the subject and smiling despite herself said she hadn't.
"Well, there were three mothers, all comparing notes on their
sons," he hastily went into the joke. "One said, 'You know, my
son, he loves me so much, he's bought me a beautiful new car.'
The second said, 'Well, my son, he's bought me a new house.'
The third said—'That's nothing! D'you want to hear what my
son does? He loves me so much that he spends an hour a day
five times a week talking to his analyst about me!'" She laughed
and gave him a hug.
   "Do you mean to tell me that's why you go and see
Dr Smythe? I didn't realise that the way I treated you in your
childhood had damaged you so much," she said ironically, and
they laughed. The front door bell rang.

"Must go," she said. "Don't worry too much about the girl-friend. You'll find another one!"

He left, commenting to himself as he did so that his mother was setting him a good example in moving on, getting over the death of her husband—and finding a new man. He liked Evan, who was folding up his rather gangling frame to fit it into his car. He was an academic like his mother, and they had a lot in common. Evan and his mother ran separate establishments, largely because Evan needed to maintain space at his house for his two children. They were in their teens and still needed a place with their father, despite being based mostly with their mother, from whom Evan was separated.

Returning to his flat, David put together some food for his supper. Generally he enjoyed cooking, but this evening he simply prepared some pasta, adding walnuts and pesto, and sat on his sofa in front of the television, glass of wine to hand. It was dark now, and he noted that the evenings were getting darker earlier now; that time of year. The autumnal coldness made him shiver suddenly. He wondered if he might be getting a cold. He felt run down and tired, chilled to the bone. Even the food and the wine did little to lift his mood but he cleared the kitchen, sluicing the plate clean in the sink, wondering if he should put the heating on. A quotation from Donne came into his mind about it's being the year's midnight, something about the shortest day, St. Lucy's day, who scarce seven hours herself unveils—or something like that. He muttered to himself that his relationship with Clara had lasted scarcely seven hours, not surprising that he felt down about it …

The phone rang suddenly, breaking his mood, and he considered leaving it to ring … he didn't feel up to dealing with a call but he made himself answer. To his surprise it was the senior therapist whom he had spoken to earlier.

"I've found a training psychotherapist for you," she said crisply, not wasting any time on conversational niceties.

"That was done very quickly," he said. "I only rang you this afternoon." She ignored this and simply gave him name and phone number. He could contact her.

David's mood lifted. For the first time since Dr Smythe's stroke he felt hopeful. A new therapy might help him to grapple with the depressions. And if he had a training therapist he would be much more likely to be accepted for training, and in his mind he saw his career progressing, blooming even. He would develop in his work, sharpen up his thinking, achieve more depth and capacity. There would be new colleagues to discuss clinical matters with, and he envisaged a bright future for himself. He felt sure that Dr Smythe would have no objection. Of course, it would be difficult to move on to a new person, having become attached to Dr Smythe, and feeling understood by him. But it couldn't be helped. And he needed to have a training therapist in order to train. Not for the first time he wondered why it was that ordinary therapists weren't good enough somehow; why was it necessary to have this special category of therapist called a training therapist?

# THREE

Meeting the new therapist was exciting on the face of it. He had asked around among his acquaintances about her reputation. The general view was that Sonya Merryn was well regarded, a kind woman. Only one person, a colleague who was a psychotherapist, sounded a note of warning. She asked him if he realised that the new psychotherapist's professional allegiance was to a particular group of therapists who did not deal with part objects. He asked her what she meant, and she explained that these therapists did not, like his Dr Smythe, think in terms of different parts of the internal world in relation to one another. In Merryn's view, and that of her colleagues, the internal world was more unitary. This set of therapists did not, like Dr Smythe and the set of therapists he belonged to, hold with the importance of very early experience in shaping the internal world. David felt uncertain, but perhaps he should give this therapist the benefit of the doubt. His experience of having approached training therapists fruitlessly made him feel he was unlikely to find one akin to Dr Smythe … psychotherapists of his set were all popular, sought after—and tended to have no vacancies.

With this in mind, he rang the number he had been given in order to arrange to meet. The Scots voice at the other end of the phone sounded neutral and very disengaged—calm—but the image came suddenly to David's mind of a heavy rock poised ready to fall from another rock on which it was precariously balanced—he had seen something like it out walking on the Cornish moors. It was a thought that he was to return to in the future, since it seemed to be a premonition, and later he wondered if he might have picked up something about the crushing negative impact this woman was likely to have on his state of mind and on his fortunes.

He arranged a time to meet, and a week later presented himself at the consulting room, upstairs in a red brick Edwardian building near the Limes clinic. The waiting room was well appointed in neutral tones, a positive jungle of indoor plants making a green tracery against one wall. Stones of various sorts rested on a table, some of them fossils, some of them agates with banding of different colours. He thought of his premonition, and hoped this therapist would not be stony in her approach. Invited into the room he saw that the therapist's couch was placed at an angle in the room rather than against a wall as he had been used to with Dr Smythe. He did not like this, feeling that any patient lying there must inevitably feel exposed and unsupported. One wall was lined with books, another with tall windows through which he could see trees in the big garden. Sonya Merryn greeted him pleasantly and indeed, as her reputation suggested, seemed a likeable person. The soft Scots burr was kind. She was a tall woman, greying, and stylishly dressed. She listened carefully and attentively to David's description of his current state, his hopes for the future, the depressions. In relation to the depressions she was more active, talking to him about them and enquiring further. She seemed a reasonable person, and David could not find any fault with her approach or what she said. However, little was made of his previous experience of therapy with Dr Smythe or the painful circumstances under which David was needing to change to a new therapist. It was only in retrospect that David noted this, and felt that he had been with someone who did not have a theoretical stance that enabled her to grasp and actively address such basic issues as this, or, indeed, the minute-by-minute shifts in the session; or who might not be able to comment with depth and focus. Anyone who did not acknowledge that, in fact, he might be unwilling to change to a different therapist seemed to be missing an important part of the beginning of the therapy, and he regretted later that he had not taken this omission seriously.

David left this introductory session having set up a four-sessions-a-week therapy, but his hopefulness had waned slightly. He shrugged off this response to his new therapist and tried to feel again as he had felt earlier, that he had a bright future. Perhaps he was still disappointed about his failure to link in with Clara? He could not tell. This sense of concern and doubt about his new therapist continued unabated over the next few months. He tried to put out of his mind his sense that he was with someone who did not have Dr Smythe's depth of understanding. He liked Sonya as a person, but as a therapist she did not seem to have any way of making sense of what her patient presented in the day-to-day run of the sessions. She did not, for example, said David to himself, comment on the beginning and end of the analytic weeks; she did not seem to notice that weekends happened and that her patient might have a particular response to the ebb and flow of the therapy around these fixed points. In his own practice David was scrupulous in observing the meaning of the breaks and interruptions in the work, and it bothered him that his therapist did not seem to be sufficiently aware of the importance of this. David found his own work beginning to suffer. He felt less sure about his stance in relation to his patients. He had one patient, Hugh, who was difficult; someone who had suffered a neglected childhood and was sent off to boarding school at the age of eight, a patient who needed the sense that his counsellor understood the impact on him of the breaks and the gaps in his twice-weekly sessions of counselling. Yet somehow David found himself less definite in his stance. His approach to the families he saw suffered similarly. He felt he had less capacity to develop an understanding of the meaning of the symptoms with which children and families came to the service.

David found the discussions he had with the child psycho-therapists around the work more meaningful than he did his discussions with his therapist. He tried to ignore the fact that the child psychotherapists adhered to the ideas of the set of psychotherapists Dr Smythe belonged to; they valued the very early experiences of their child patients in making sense of their difficulties, and this made sense to David too. One family in particular, about whom he had previously felt certain in his clinical formulations, began to seem more difficult to under-stand and help. He thought this was to do with the work with his own therapist meandering on rather meaninglessly.

This was a one-parent family. The daughter, Petra, aged nine, had remained hospitalised straight after birth because of severe problems and had needed major surgery. As described by her mother, Wilma, there had been great anxiety about whether she would survive, and anxiety continued to be a feature of her childhood. At nursery her mother was asked to keep her at home after a few months, as she would become floppy and breathless, her problems still very apparent. She worried the nursery staff, who felt anxious about collapse. At the age of seven she had further surgery, and returned to school, but by the age of nine she was finding it difficult to leave her mother to attend school at all. Belatedly, in David's view, she was offered weekly sessions of child psychotherapy, and David offered sessions at the same time to her mother. The aim of the work was to help Wilma and her daughter to separate so that Petra could return to school, addressing the anxiety and making sense of it. Petra was a slight girl, with light-coloured hair and a transparency of skin that seemed to heighten a sense of the nine-year-old not really being solidly there; she avoided relating. Eye contact was minimal and she clung to her mother.

The initial three-session assessment was done by David, working with a child psychotherapy colleague who was very skilled and extremely busy as a clinician. Simon made it clear that he liked having to work with David. He was a mild-mannered man with a lined and rather squashed-looking face and light-brown hair which stuck up like a close set of bristles. His work overload made conversation difficult. At the start of the therapy they ran into the separation problem immediately, when Petra refused to stay in the room with Simon and ran hastily and anxiously back to her mother in the room where David was working, flinging open the door, rushing at her mother and hiding behind her. Wilma seemed to feel that this was somehow Simon's fault. Previously David would have had no difficulty in thinking about this as a separation problem, underpinned by the early difficulties and anxieties about Petra's health, but he felt uncertain and unsure about how to proceed. Should he and Simon work separately, in parallel as usual, in different rooms? Or together with mother and daughter in the same room? He felt his stance in the work was undermined by his doubts about what he was doing in his own therapy and his difficulty in understanding Sonya's stance, which although kind, was rather silent and vague.

He also felt that his work with his colleague was undermined by the difficulty in finding time to discuss it. He knew that Simon was very busy, caught up with a paper he was writing, and occupying a senior role in the service with responsibility for supervising younger clinicians. David could not argue that the difficulties he found in creating time for discussion with his colleague were difficulties that related to the case—it was much more that Simon clearly had very little time. David noticed that Simon was very active in case discussion meetings, with some very sound thinking, so he decided to bring the case, with Simon's agreement, to one of the weekly meetings. Here the team met to discuss difficult cases with each other, with the focus on how best to move the work forward in a constructive way. David found these meetings very helpful indeed and it was a source of satisfaction to him that he could contribute some cogent ideas to the discussions. On this occasion the discussion about the case was lively, and Simon and he were able to get to grips with some of its dynamics. After the meeting David felt very pleased that he had taken the step of bringing the case to the team for discussion. With the help of the team, he and Simon agreed to work separately, since Petra was now able to stay with Simon in the room. This seemed to work reasonably well except for the paucity of clinical discussion about the case. David was used to having helpful clinical discussions with colleagues after and before sessions, and he noticed that his colleague was still too busy. Sighing to himself, he had to admit that the dynamics in this situation were not to do with the case, but to do with the reality of the actual situation. There was a profound shortage of clinical staff, and David found himself suggesting in a staff meeting that the team should focus on this issue and develop an action plan to address it. The idea was thrown around in a general way until David noticed that both the child psychiatrist and the principal clinical psychologist were very taken with the idea of doing a study of the number of cases taken on in the team, and the extent to which families were required to wait until one of the clinicians became available to provide the appropriate therapeutic input. Sometimes the waits could be extremely lengthy, and there was pressure to take on more work than each clinician could really manage. This had been raised with management before and the response then had been the same as ever: not enough resources to make it possible to appoint more staff to deal with the workload. This time the idea of compiling careful statistics, suggested by David, found favour and an action plan was agreed.

One of the cats lay in the room, snoozing during the conversation. David thought about the public's view that current levels of taxation provided enough support for healthcare, and how this was rather similar to the cat's sleep. He had to make an effort to remind himself that he was there to do the work, and he would be wasting energy if he allowed himself to be caught up in frustration at the lack of staff. His therapist commented later, with accuracy, that he might find the general lack of resourcing difficult in view of his experience of his father's emotional unavailability, and David had to admit to himself that this was a helpful comment.

The presence of the cat was echoed by a dog's presence when David went for his therapy later. He arrived at the front door to see the flimsy gate beside it rattling on its hinges under the assault of a dog on the other side, barking loudly and trying to get through the wood, which was silvery grey in the parts that were not covered with peeling green paint. A sign saying "Tradesman's entrance" was just discernible. He flinched, feeling already stressed by the events of the day, but gritted his teeth, and, ignoring the idea that the aged gate might give way and that he would be ferociously attacked, went into the building. In his session he started by way of referring to his experience that it was as well that the dog had not been an incarnation of the Hound of the Baskervilles, getting through the gate and attacking him.

Sonya, surprised that anyone could find her barking dog disconcerting, laughed and said "Oh, he was just saying hello!" David grimaced to himself. This was, of course, probably the reality of the situation: the dog had been barking a greeting. But as usual he felt that this comment, whilst accurate and even amusing, omitted any attempt to address the significance of his reaction and what he had said, which would have provided a way in to understanding his internal world. As usual, he did not feel that his therapist's comment was directed at elucidating meaning, while Dr Smythe would have waited until a theme in the session emerged, and made some comment that would have done so. On this occasion, as on many others, David was left to think about the meaning of his feelings by himself, without any helpful input from Sonya.

He wondered about the fact that he was angry about the resourcing of the team, a feeling he had been struggling with that day. Could he have lodged those feelings in the dog, experiencing him in a paranoid way as likely to launch a savage attack? If Dr Smythe had been dealing with the session, he might have made a comment tactfully linking his ideas with his feeling about the weekend break (it happened to be a Monday). Or he might have linked his feeling of lack of progress in his team's attempt to resolve funding difficulties with his experience in the incubator, which he felt, as a tiny baby, to be life destructive and attacking rather than sustaining. David could think that the family dynamic, with his father's withdrawal, was also represented in his experience of the team that he felt was so understaffed. Or was it that he felt likely to be attacked verbally by Sonya? This would certainly fit in with his experience of her frequent silences as stony if not critical. At the end of the session Sonya's usual way of ending the session—"Time's up for today"—seemed to David to have the withdrawn manner of someone who had not been listening, who had not heard a word of what he was saying, of someone with no capacity to tease out meaning. He felt he had been left to flounder in a welter of possible meanings without any containing guidance. His therapist had stayed with the flippant comment, without doing any work to try to make sense of her patient's experience.

David was still suffering from the double effect of the day and of his session when he got to the choir in which he sang on Monday evenings. As usual his state of mind was very much improved as they rehearsed some Purcell. He loved the clarity of line in Purcell's music. And as usual he admired the soprano with the high clear voice who stood just in front of him where he sang tenor. And, as usual, the sight of her made him think about Clara. He occasionally saw Clara in the distance at meetings, and he was still hopeful of connecting with her.

# FOUR

At the weekend David went for a run with Jack. Jack was in an excited state of mind, eyes gleaming as they ran past the café, which was full of families and couples on such a fine sunny morning. His golden hair was lit up almost into a halo by the sun behind, as he confided, beside himself with excitement, that he had been accepted to train at the Radcliffe as a psychotherapist. David was not surprised.

"I'm pleased for you, Jack," he said breathlessly—they were running at a speed to match Jack's elevated mood.

"Yes, great, isn't it? You should apply too, you know. They would be very enthusiastic about someone like you applying."

"I'm really not sure about that. I went and had an introductory chat and the response was less than enthusiastic ... in fact I had the distinct impression that the person I saw was trying to dissuade me ... What were your interviews like?"

"The interviews weren't too bad, really. I was expecting something much more searching. I kind of got the impression that I wasn't quite waved through but there was rather that feeling ... I think being a medic helps." By unspoken mutual consent they stopped at a spot where they could look from the hill over the city. Puffy white clouds cast shadows on the grass and the sun had a welcome brightness. In the blue distance

David could see the hills beyond the clusters of tall buildings that gleamed white and geometric in the clear air.

"I think I might find it more difficult to be accepted than you, not being a medic," David said.

"Well it's worth a try," said Jack. "Come on," and he dashed off again downhill. David ran after him, feet thudding down the path.

Jack's success made David feel that it was worth pursuing an application. He got an application form and filled it in carefully, puzzling over what he should say about himself. Unlike Dr Smythe, his therapist was, he felt, not so much neutral about his application as negative, but not in any way that he could put his finger on. David just felt that when he raised it with her as a possibility her response was not an active one, and she did not really make any comment at all, either positive or negative. Nor did she link his wish to train with his positive feelings about the therapy, as Dr Smythe had done. David felt that he was pursuing a course of action about which his therapist had no views at all; Sonya made the analytic silence seem persecutory and David was not quite sure how to read her. He had got used to the fact that Sonya did not make eye contact with him or say hello when he arrived for the session. He supposed that analytic neutrality dictated that there would be no comment about the actuality of his wish to train, but he wondered at Sonya's failure to discuss it in any real way. She did ask questions about his plans for the timing of the application and so on, but that was all. David felt that his intention was viewed negatively but, as usual, the negativity and disapproval was something that was in the atmosphere in the room rather than articulated clearly.

It was spring before he had the dates of his two interviews for the training. As he walked towards the first one, a black cat crossed his path and he laughed to himself, remembering what Jack had said, supportively, when David had seen a black cat on his way to an interview in the past. "I had my envoys out," he had said. A buoyant sense of Jack being alongside him in a humorous way lessened the anxiety he felt. This first interview was with a psychotherapist called Paul French. The atmosphere in his consulting room reminded David of Victorian novels he had read: the walls were a sheeny dark grey, the couch had a coverlet of some darker velvet, and the light from two table lamps was muted. The light coming from the street was blocked out so that there was a sense of womb-like dimness. Paul French was a short man dressed in a tweed jacket, fair hair tinged with grey. He smiled with some warmth, and David liked him immediately, which he felt was a good sign. Perhaps the feeling would be reciprocated and he would be accepted to train. Paul French listened carefully as he explained that he would like to train as a psychotherapist to enhance his clinical capacity, to ensure that he was clinically as competent as he could be in his practice. This seemed to meet with some approval, but what was less approved was the smallness of his private practice as a counsellor. Paul French expressed some doubts about his identity as a clinician, since his main work was in the family consultation service. David protested that it was in order to move over into a more psychotherapeutic identity that he was seeking to train, but was met with a doubtful look.

David ventured then to talk about his family background, his early experiences; the extent to which therapy had helped him. Paul French said little until David mentioned his depression at Oxford. He asked him to elaborate on what had happened. David explained that he had been low, depressed, and felt that his move into adult life away from home had been difficult, his efforts to move on not founded on solidity … Paul French asked him if at that time he had felt that life wasn't worth living and David remembered, with an acute pain, his sense of feeling that indeed he didn't have a life that he wanted, that he had really been struggling. He explained carefully to Paul French that at that time—and he was careful to locate the experience firmly in the past—he had felt quite down. Paul French asked if he had acted on those feelings. David hesitated and then decided to be truthful. He had, in fact, driven his car with a degree of carelessness which was quite life-threatening. He had been involved in an accident. He had overtaken a car on a blind bend crossing a bridge; another car coming in the other direction had run into him. He had some minor injuries and his car was written off, but the other driver was unhurt. He had spent several days getting over the injuries of that accident ... but nobody had guessed what he himself knew, that he had not been paying proper attention to his driving. He laughed at his student carelessness and accident proneness but Paul French did not laugh; in fact he seemed to latch on to the event.

Paul French asked him how he understood now, in retrospect, what had happened. David hesitated. He felt that he would rather not be talking about this incident, and in such depth about his feelings at university. It was not current, he felt; not relevant. This was an interview for a professional training, not a clinical interview as a psychotherapy assessment. Reluctantly he said that now, when he looked back, he felt that he could relate his low mood of that time of his life to his father's state of mind, his suicide ... the question had been how to be a successful person with this role model in the family, and of course there was the prematurity that he described too ... he hastily added that his father had been professionally very successful ... he had written books about the subtleties of interpreting, and in the field of linguistics. Paul French interposed quickly.

"But he did kill himself."

David wondered why he was being pressed on this point. He himself was a successful person now, not like the depressed and fraught student he had been in those years at Oxford.

He barely thought about that time now. Then his sense of unsteadiness came vividly back to him; his difficulty in focusing on the work, his sense of alienation, his unhappiness when a girlfriend broke up with him.

"I think you're trying to make a case that there's something questionable about me because my father killed himself," he phrased what he said carefully. "My situation now's very different from the situation I was struggling with at Oxford. I have a successful life."

"Well, it's bound to have had some lingering effect, your family circumstances, don't you think?" Paul French said smoothly. The invitation was to dwell on those difficult years. David insisted that those experiences had in some sense been beneficial. He had been impelled to seek help and to reflect on his state of mind, and this had been useful. He had not been prevented from training himself as a counsellor and as a psychologist. In fact, he remarked with some asperity, he felt that those difficult experiences had given him some depth and had forced him to think about his internal world, a process that he felt could only benefit his current as well as his future patients.

"I do think you are rather minimising those experiences," Paul French said in a concerned way, as though, David thought with some irritation, he might be talking as a clinician, rather than someone interviewing an applicant for a training.

David wondered why it was that Paul French seemed determined to see him as a patient rather than as a putative psychotherapist, someone who was already a clinician with a lot to offer. He barely had time to engage with this idea before he was being asked about his name.

"What does it mean, in English?" asked Paul French.

"Treuherz? It means true heart," said David. He felt that somehow the interview had been derailed by a focus on his difficulties. To his amazement he now found that Paul French was suggesting that he might consider changing his name.

"It's an invitation to over-closeness," he remarked. David did not know what to say. This seemed so extraordinary a thought, and so far from what he might think of doing, that it seemed a very odd proposition. He muttered something about this not having been a difficulty in the past with patients he had seen nor in his work as a clinical psychologist. He wondered how, in all seriousness, such a proposition could be made. Was the Radcliffe the sort of institution in which intending acolytes had to be remade in a new image? He was attached to his name; it was what he had of his father.

"It's just a thought," said Paul French, clearly seeing that he had shocked him with this comment. "But, look, you are going to have a second interview … and of course, we'll do what we can for you. We need to stop there."

David got back into his car surprised, if not irritated. When he had been sent off with the parting comment, "We'll do what we can for you", the impression that he had been dismissed like a patient rather than an intending trainee was strengthened. He was surprised at the stance taken. How was it that he had allowed Paul French to focus so much on his early difficulties, as an infant as well as a student, rather than on his accomplishments? Surely an English degree from Oxford, admittedly not a First, was to be reckoned with, would provide some sort of solid foundation from which to apply to the Radcliffe? Was it that his father's suicide and his own low mood as a twenty-year-old debarred him? He felt that the interview had been unsatisfactory, having as it did such a clinical focus. And to be told that he should change his name! This seemed intolerably overweening on his interviewer's part, and when he told Jack about it the next day Jack crowed delightedly.

"Don't you see, David?" he asked laughing. "These people are all clinicians. They don't *know* how to manage an interview that isn't clinical!"

"Did you find the same in your interviews?" asked David. "Seriously."

"No, I didn't ... but as I keep saying to you, I'm a medic and that's almost a passport ... as long as I can walk and talk, I'm in ... They're keen to have medics who seem competent ... Look, put it behind you, you've got another interview where you can convey a good impression ... Impress by your capacity for self-reflection ... Come to dinner on Saturday, I'm inviting some people. You'll enjoy it."

Saturday was one of those early spring days when the sun is dazzlingly warm, the sky a washed pale blue, and the fluffy white clouds have something of summer about them. David went for a solitary walk in the park. Approaching a lake he saw a cormorant diving, and was puzzled by the sight. A sea bird seemed out of keeping here, with blackbirds beginning to make the air delightful with fluid trills and piercingly sweet tones, and green parakeets squawking and darting overhead. As he sat on a bench by the lake in the warm sun, the cormorant surfaced with a large fish in its beak, which it began to force down its throat. Fascinated, David watched until every vestige of the unfortunate fish had disappeared and the cormorant gulped blackly, stretching out its wings. There was something gruesome yet fascinating about the determination of the bird to force the fish down its throat. David thought ahead to Jack's dinner. Jack had recently started living with his girlfriend, a friend and colleague of Clara's, who was also a psychologist. He thought with some pleasure though, that there would be a lot of shop talked. But he would see Clara—with Georg.

Later that day David found himself seated in Jack's living room whilst a selection of people he knew and half knew chatted animatedly around him. He knew Jack's new partner, of course, a woman who reminded him of the child psychotherapist he worked with. The difference was that Jack's partner Marie was French, a gawky blonde woman whose slow manner and stylish dress concealed a brightness of mind that David had found impressive when they met. She was also at the Limes clinic but unlike Jack had not taken the step of applying to the Radcliffe. Not yet, said David to himself as he watched her talking and laughing with Georg and Clara. He thought of Jack and Marie as a starry couple with their golden hair and their liveliness. David thought how wonderful it was to see Clara, even though she seemed linked with Georg. To David's distaste he found himself seated opposite Georg at the dining table. He need not have worried. Georg addressed one remark to him, designed to elicit whether or not he was at the Radcliffe, and having established that he was not, made no further remark to him, focusing his conversational efforts on Jack and two other people who were already well on with their training at the Radcliffe. David listened in some amazement as he told story after story focusing on his excellence as a clinician. He imagined he could detect an expression in Clara's eyes that indicated that she found his tendency to self-aggrandisement wearing and rather unpleasant.

He hoped it wasn't just wishful thinking on his part. He focused on the food. Marie was proud of her cooking, and had produced a chestnut soup followed by fish baked in parcels with lemon and sage and tiny new potatoes swimming in butter as an accompaniment. The pudding she apologised for, since it was another chestnut dish, this time a chestnut puree dotted with tiny meringues and dollops of cream.

"Delicious, Marie," he said, and engaged her in conversation about music. They were both in the choir and he knew that she was passionate about the music that he also loved: Byrd, Tallis, the sort of music they often sang. Try as he might, though, he could not blot out Georg's steady tones telling yet another story about some supervision he had done which he was holding out as a model of excellence. He glimpsed Clara and for a moment their eyes met and he could tell she was somewhat embarrassed by Georg's extravagance. Perhaps he had drunk a little too much. They had coffee in Jack's large lounge furnished in delicate shades of white and fashionable grey. David decided he could see Marie's hand in the choice of style.

David sought to establish himself next to Clara. She was as attractive as ever. She looked well, colour in her animated face, wearing a close-fitting dress in shades of apricot and green that set off her green eyes and the green jade necklace and drop earrings she was wearing. He thought that the word to describe her was bewitching, and he fell gratefully under her spell. She seemed genuinely pleased to see him, and he told her of his application and the interview he had just had. He could see that she was impressed by the fact that he had applied and she reminded him that she too was applying, but had heard nothing despite having been interviewed some months previously. He felt suddenly competitive—she was certain to be accepted as she was so obviously intelligent and accomplished. He turned the conversation and asked her about her mother's health. She was touched that he remembered her concern about her mother, and said that she was well now, she had recovered, there had been worry but it was over now. He was preternaturally aware of how close she was as she sat on the sofa next to him.

She was surprised that he hadn't known that Georg had moved in with her. Carefully toneless, he said he hadn't known. He recovered somewhat from the shock of the news, and with something of a mischievous edge and twinkle remarked that Georg seemed to be very experienced. He must have a lot to offer her in terms of thinking about her cases; she might not need to pay a supervisor for her psychotherapy work—she had one at home. She blushed slightly, detecting the irony in his tone, and shortly afterwards moved away from him, ostensibly in search of more coffee. He was annoyed with himself for having allowed his true feeling about Georg to show through in this slightly biting way; of course he was edgy about him; Georg had stolen Clara away from him almost from under his nose; but he also disliked Georg's obviously rather grand view of himself. He resented the fact that Georg so clearly favoured the company of Radcliffe people. It was a relief to David when the party broke up, but he smiled at Jack as he left.

"Nice party, Jack, thanks, you and Marie must come to me next time. Lovely food, Marie—love the chestnuts!" She laughed, enjoying his teasing tone and gave him a warm parting kiss on both cheeks.

He walked home, the warmth of the wine slowly ebbing and leaving him cold and his mood irritable. Rat race, he muttered to himself. Georg—stupid egotist. So competitive. And what for? Why did he need to puff himself up like that? He had the woman, he had the Radcliffe … David was upset that Georg had so clearly ignored him. He wondered how long Clara would tolerate his overblown manner. Not long, he hoped, and this was a thought to comfort himself with as he let himself into his flat.

His mood was a little improved when he went into the service the next day and met his child psychotherapy colleague just before their appointment with the family they were seeing together. Simon told him that the mother, Wilma, had left a message that morning to say that Petra had been at school all the previous week. She would like to see David for their usual appointment, but Petra would not be coming as she was at school. They would need to arrange another appointment time, and she would like to do that to enable Petra to avoid missing school.

"Good news, Simon!" Jack said. In keeping with the collegial warmth developing between them, the harassed Simon permitted himself a smile. They compared diaries and found a time when they could see Petra and her mother Wilma after school.

As he sat down with Wilma, David could hear the wind in the branches of the tree outside his window. He liked the dark green of the tree, and he had noticed the blackbirds in the bushes near it, and the waxy red berries made a contrast with the dark green of the holly and the bright yellow beaks of the blackbirds. Not for the first time he wondered how it was that they could make so much noise rustling in the bushes, and how they could eat berries that he had thought were poisonous. The colours reminded him of medieval paintings and he allowed this thought to engage his mind for a moment before he turned his attention firmly to Wilma.

Wilma was a thin, careworn woman who was looking pleased today, conscious that something of a corner had been turned in that she had managed to get Petra to school. "What made the difference, then, do you think?" asked David, pleased that there seemed to be some signs of Petra being able to get to school despite her mother's anxiety. And indeed, Petra's anxiety about her mother. Wilma was chronically depressed, and gave David the impression that she needed to have Petra there at home with her as a partner, a substitute for Petra's father who had left during the early years of Petra's life. David guessed that during those early years the parental couple would have needed extraordinary emotional capacity to bear with the anguish of possibly losing their first child. On the other hand, Wilma was someone who had failed to separate from her own parents, and he imagined that Petra's father might have had to be a person of some magnetism to attract Wilma to himself, and away from them.

"It was the school and the visit you made there," Wilma explained, characteristically giving the credit for the change to the school, and himself. "They arranged a learning mentor for Petra. Petra liked her straight away. As long as she's able to give her one-to-one attention, it's manageable." David felt concerned about this as the basis for Petra going back. While the learning mentor could focus on her individually, Petra would indeed be likely to cope. But in David's experience, learning mentors and teaching assistants tended to be spread amongst groups of children, and Petra would be lucky to have this level of support for very long. He tried to say something of this to Wilma and he saw her eyes glaze over as she failed to take in his point. He decided not to pursue the issue when she returned to a subject they had talked about before, her own experience of school.

Wilma had struggled in separating from her mother and settling in school, since she had been concerned about her mother's safety in the home; her father had been a violent, impulsive man from whom she felt she needed to protect her mother. Her mother had needed her to be at home in order to provide support and to be a buffer against her father. Wilma had attended school sporadically, spending her time with her mother and grandmother, and by secondary school was hardly attending at all. David felt that his providing a point of stability, support, and attachment for her would be necessary in order for her to develop some ability to let Petra go. It would be increasingly important as Petra moved into adolescence and the crucial task of taking on her own life. It was a crucial period for them to be getting help. David's regret was the difficulty in working with Simon, and he tried to think of ways of linking in with him more so that they could work together more helpfully. At least the family were having the vitally necessary long-term work.

He wondered aloud to Wilma whether Petra felt the need to support her mother at home, in much the same way that she felt she had needed to support her own mother. Perhaps it was difficult for Petra to feel that Wilma was getting on with some activity of her own. But if she were able to, it would help Petra feel that she was safely leaving at home a mother who was getting on with her own life whilst she was at school. What had she been interested in at school? He got as far as hearing about her interest in art before she managed to turn the conversation back to Petra and the horrors of her early days. Post-traumatic stress, thought David to himself, and as usual he wondered why it was that hospitals were only now really beginning to realise that parents might need emotional support to help them work through the shock and impact of having to deal with sick children. He talked to her about her fear of her violent father. It might seem to her that there had in some sort of way been a violent attack on the baby Petra as she was so terribly ill, and this experience of ordinary well-being, good health, and emotional stability being attacked might have made her very vulnerable at that time. Sighing to himself he allowed her once more to run through this dreadful experience, and carefully made a link for her which he hoped she would find meaningful in this new situation. Could it be that she experienced Petra beginning to separate from her, starting to go back to school, as likely to be catastrophic, a violent attack on her, rather like her experience giving birth to her, that first separation, and the devastating ill health she had suffered as a baby?

Wilma considered this in silence. The blackbirds clucked in the bushes outside. Inside the building he heard a teenager finishing his session with one of the psychotherapists. He clattered down the stairs, clearly racing to be away out of the building and far from whatever discomfort he had felt in his session. He wondered about the sound-proofing and whether this could be improved. He noticed the trend of his thinking and realised how difficult it was to stay focused on Wilma and wondered if this could be significant. Could this be a reflection of her own mother's difficulty in holding her in mind, focusing on her? Had her mother been very preoccupied with her marital problems? Had Wilma been rather ignored, leading her to cling to her mother, to fail to separate from her, just as her own daughter Petra could not separate from her? Wilma stirred, looking up from the floor she had been contemplating, and he saw that her eyes had tears in them.

"I'm really hoping that Petra can stay at school," she said. "I feel that with you helping me, and Simon helping Petra as well as the learning mentor, there is some hope." Then she shrugged and said, "The school have got to make an effort to keep the learning mentor focused on her, just her. It'll be no use if the mentor goes and gets involved with other kids." "I agree," David said. "She needs to settle into school, feel confident there, before the learning mentor is withdrawn. Do you think you could say something like that to her teacher?" Wilma nodded, but he had the sense that she might avoid doing this so that the promising change would be undermined. One part of her actively wanted Petra to attend school, but another more ambivalent part of her might be quite unwilling to work towards a goal that involved separation from her. It was no easy matter to overcome the difficulties of her own early life, to have to pick up the threads of her life, properly, for the first time, and to move on and to be separate from the daughter who had come to represent a stable presence in her life. They agreed that Wilma would talk to the teacher about the need for the teaching mentor to provide maximum support for Petra in the first weeks of starting back at school. Again, David felt that long-term work was very necessary with this complex family.

It was the end of the session and almost the end of day. David knew that Simon would probably run his next child patient's session very closely to the end of Petra's and that there wouldn't be time for them to think through the sessions together. He jotted down his own notes, and made the laborious entry on the computer system to show that Wilma had attended with her daughter. As usual he lamented the fact that the computer system had no capacity to enter two appointments, one with the child and one with the parent with two different clinicians; he had to fill in the diary as though the child patient was the focus, and the work with the parent was not significant in any way. It was an issue he raised frequently but somehow it didn't seem possible for the change to be made to the computer system. To his mind this represented something very old-fashioned about the service: the child was viewed as the patient and was treated as an individual, despite the fact that so many of the difficulties related to the position of the child in the family—and in the mind of each of the parents—and in the parents' history, both as a couple and individually.

# FIVE

The next day there was the second interview for the Radcliffe training to address. He arrived promptly at the small terraced house where his next interviewer had her consulting room. He rang the bell and the psychotherapist came to the door and opened it. He said hello and she greeted this with a blank face and stiff nod. A young woman with blonde hair, she was slim—and, to his discomfort, determinedly silent. He looked around her consulting room for a moment as he wondered how to deal with the fact that she wasn't going to say anything. He noticed the plants, again, the neutral setting, the couch, the rather graceful antique furniture with which the room was furnished. He decided he would volunteer first of all why he wanted to train at the Radcliffe, and discussed his wish to enhance his clinical capacity and the fact that it was the obvious place to approach to do so. She greeted this with another stiff nod, and said nothing. Saffra Downy had a good reputation—but she didn't seem to speak.

He decided that he would tell her about himself and gave a brief description of the path he had taken in applying to the interview. He described his prematurity, and family life. His father, his mother, the move from Switzerland to England. As he described his move to England the experience came vividly to life in his mind. They had taken a train to get the boat from Hook of Holland, an overnight sailing. His mother had bought him a new toy to play with on the train to occupy him while she endeavoured to manage his little sisters. He remembered his delight with the little cork mat the box held, along with a brightly coloured wooden hammer and a selection of little pins. The shapes the box contained—circles, semi-circles, triangles, squares—were also wooden, smooth and painted in bright primary colours—yellow, red, blue, green. Each had a little hole in the middle and he industriously set to work to make patterns by hammering the little pins into the shapes. Tap, tap. The journey flew by. He remembered suddenly the other toys he'd had in Switzerland, like the board game called *"Flieg mein Hütchen"*, which involved little plastic hats, again in primary colours, that could be catapulted through the air by a little see-saw to land on the gaming board.

He remembered walking up the gangplank into the ship, which had seemed huge, looming above him in the darkness; he could only just grasp the idea that it *was* a ship. After an unsettled night in a cabin in which the floor moved (inexplicably to his mind) up and down, arriving in Harwich the next morning, to be greeted by his mother's family, seemed dreamlike. He wrenched himself back to the present—was it, once again, an experience of being somehow infantilised that was generating these memories of his early life? Rather stiffly he carried on describing his family to this silent woman. His sisters: one now a watercolour painter, the other an academic, with a speciality in mediaeval history. He described his own choice to study English. This all took half an hour and, to his amazement, she had said nothing. He knew, from her attentiveness and the little nods she gave, that she was listening, but she did not speak.

He was then taken aback when she did finally speak, just like his previous interviewer, about the difficult year he had spent at Oxford. She enquired in great detail about what he had experienced at that time and what he now made of that experience. He tried to demonstrate thoughtfulness and a capacity for self-reflection and he did feel for a while that he was with a person who was responsive and not unsympathetic. It was, however, entirely unclear to him whether she agreed or not with his view that the despondency and difficulty he had experienced during his Oxford year had been very helpful in providing him with an entrée into his later career. He asserted again that he had needed to think about his internal world, the influences on it from the external experiences he had lived through, and what he might have brought to the experience himself. He talked about his prematurity, his early experiences, feeling that this was relevant. As he left the interview he did not feel that he had provided a picture of himself as a thoughtful person. It was so difficult to get any sort of dialogue going. It was not a surprise to him when he got a letter some three months later (slow time at the Radcliffe, Jack had said) rejecting his application and inviting him to meet with one of his interviewers if he so chose. He did choose, interested to see what feedback he might get. He was not hopeful, and indeed attended a meeting with Paul French without any expectation.

Paul French said very little other than to tell him that he thought he did not have a strong enough sense of identity as a psychologist, and that perhaps he should really think seriously of changing his name. However, when David asked him directly about when he should reapply, he did suggest that David should do so in about two years' time. This, he said, would be about right.

It was a further shock to David to find that Clara had been accepted. He did not know what to make of his friends being accepted whilst he wasn't. Clearly, in Jack's case he was a medic, but in Clara's case? She was a psychologist, and she was the same age … but did it make a difference that she was living with a psychotherapist? Already part of the charmed circle, perhaps? Of course he did not suggest this to her face when they happened to meet shortly after he had been turned down and she had been accepted … but he did mull over the fact that he was a clinical psychologist and a counsellor from a fringe organisation whilst she was a psychologist and had a doctorate. He had to acknowledge to himself that this looked better. And she had a therapy with one of the group of therapists to which Dr Smythe belonged, with their helpful focus on infantile experience. The child as father to the man. That would certainly enhance her capacity to reflect on herself with the early years in mind, giving more depth to her discussion of her own inner world in the interview.

Since his application to the Radcliffe had been rejected David tried to enhance his career in other ways. He undertook a baby observation seminar at the Limes clinic—he had not undertaken a seminar of this sort as part of his psychology training. He enjoyed the seminar, which met weekly with a senior clinician to discuss the observation of the babies and to tease out meaning from the observed hour of interaction between mother and baby. The idea was to enhance observational capacity in the young clinicians, and David found himself enlivened in these seminars. Less easy and more challenging, however, was the weekly observation of a new mother and her baby, and he had to deal with the feelings stirred up in him by the situation. The mother he observed was well supported by her husband and her own family, and she was able to maintain a stance of being focused on her baby. Touchingly, she was preoccupied with the material setting for him, providing him and herself with large numbers of outfits. She was good at structuring their life together, frequently taking him out to mother-and-baby groups and getting into a settled routine with him at home. He thought the baby thrived. He found writing up the minute-by-minute observation of the hour's activities and the feeling tone of the situation arduous, especially when the baby was asleep, but found the discussion in the seminar thoughtful and felt that his own capacity for thought and reflection was improving as a result.

## SIX

As though the disappointment with the Radcliffe and with Clara was not enough to struggle with, David suddenly had much more with which to contend.

Like his father, David's mother liked to swim, generally in the sea. She and Evan were in the habit of spending their holidays in Cornwall, where they would walk, swim, and deal with some of the reading and writing of papers they didn't have time to attend to during term time. During the academic year she took little exercise apart from a weekend country walk, and would admit that she was envious of David's running and of the fact that Evan was also a runner and a cyclist, riding his bicycle to work routinely. So her heart attack was something that perhaps should have been expected; she had seemed more tired in the months preceding the summer and had talked with enthusiasm of her retirement planned for the following year. The workload she undertook had been heavy.

That summer, temporarily (he hoped) single, David had joined his mother and stepfather for a week and joined in their walks and swims, enjoying the break in his routine and glad of the chance to get away. He planned to join friends in a cottage in Brittany after he had returned to London, spending a week back at work and then going on leave again. However, one evening during that week in London, as he was cooking himself a meal, Evan rang, speaking calmly despite being clearly distraught. There had been no warning, nothing. David's mother had a heart attack as they were climbing a steep coastal path near the beach. The lifeguards had been magnificent. The air ambulance had been called and took her to hospital but it was such a massive heart attack there was nothing they could do.

David passed that week in a state of disbelief and shock. He shook his head when Evan remarked that she would have found retirement difficult.

"But she had so many plans, Evan!" he said, and then found it too painful to run through the ideas that his mother had been talking over with him only a week ago. He wondered if she had suffered much. He wasn't sure if people who had heart attacks felt much pain. He hoped not. Evan clearly suffered: effective and single-minded in making the necessary arrangements for the funeral, he was pale, thin-lipped, and withdrawn.

The funeral was an ordeal. Those colleagues and friends who were in London, rather than away for the summer, crowded the chapel and stood tearful and disbelieving at the graveside. David was reminded of his father's funeral, his mother's brave words in the eulogy. This time it was Evan who spoke; David and his sisters read poems and passages that seemed appropriate. He thought the words from Heine's poem about the new spring giving back what the winter had taken away were effective, although almost unbearably poignant. Once people are taken away, he thought wretchedly, later in his flat while preparing a meal for his sister and her boyfriend, they aren't given back. Not like the seasons; *they* come round again and again. People just disappear. Memories of them inhabit our minds, he thought, but their physical presence has gone. He was glad that his mother, at Evan's insistence, was buried rather than cremated. He treasured the idea that she still had a physical presence, even if in the grave. He suddenly remembered a German colleague of his mother's, arriving back after his holiday, being told the news and his aghast face and his shock, and his insistence as he asked, "*Aber—wo ist das Grab?*"—"Where is the grave?" He had slipped into German in the stress of the moment. It was a comfort to be able to take him to the spot, to take flowers there. With ashes, as with his father's death, there was nothing left. Ashes could be scattered, but they disappeared. Tears came to his eyes and he wiped them hurriedly aside, focusing as best he might on the food he was making. His sister Susie came into the kitchen and seeing his tearfulness gave him a hug. The live warmth of her blonde hair brushed his cheek.

"Awful, isn't it? I can't believe it," she said. "Here, let me help you with that," and she took the spoon from him and began to stir the fragrant sauce he was making. His mother had taught him to cook. He felt cold and nauseous. He could not believe it either. How could this happen? It was so sudden. He talked to Susie and her boyfriend over dinner, and the sporadic conversation was a painful one. Susie painted delicate watercolours, and she had brought him one as a gift—pale-looking flowers in a glass jar, the colours melting over the boundaries of the lines like tears that had dried. The jar was beautifully delineated, the water accurately refracting the stems of the flowers, the disjunction as their stems entered the water. He found himself talking about the way that so many cultures did not allow for the finality of death; there was a paradise or a heaven or a place where the shades wandered, as in Greek myth. It's a comforting defence, said the psychologist in him, and Matthew, Susie's stonemason husband, said that even the monuments at gravesides had to be hewn out of stone, to last, to provide a continuity and a refusal to accept the ultimate separation of death. David found himself moved by the conversation. They could acknowledge their grief together. It didn't have to be denied, and he was grateful for that. Grateful for the fact that he wasn't an only child, coping alone with the terrible feeling of loss that assailed him.

He joined his friends the week after he had originally intended to go, and took long solitary walks on the cliffs and beaches. He missed his ex-girlfriend. He felt alone, despite the warmth and support of his friends. He supposed, drearily, that this was all necessary. He had mourned his father. Now he had to mourn his mother. It was a miserable few weeks and he was glad to get back to work, to focus on the difficulties of the families and his patients. At the weekends he visited the grave, taking flowers, thinking he should have taken her more flowers when she was alive. He regretted his single-mindedness about his career, his life, his girlfriend and the lack of time he'd had for her.

His therapist was clearly shocked and sympathetic. David became depressed. Very down. Sonya had little to say, and David found her less than helpful; more accusatory than anything else as the weeks of therapy passed and David continued in his miserable state. The summer months had gone and the year was inclining again towards autumn. David fell into the habit of walking in the park by himself, looking greyly at the colours that flamed in a burst of brilliance on the trees and were gradually extinguished as the winter cold set in. The gaunt black branches of the trees dripping in the November dullness suited his mood. The dank air and the cold rain chilled him through and through. That winter it seemed not to get light at all. He tried to combat his interior darkness by lighting his flat brilliantly with extra side lamps but nothing seemed to shake his mood. He found that his work was the only source of comfort, until Sonya commented one day, in what felt like critical mode, that he was lodging his distress in his patients and the families he saw and was looking after it there. David felt that this might be right, as a comment on his current plight, but it was less than helpful. He found the work sustained him, blotting out, necessarily, his own distress as he focused carefully on what was brought to the sessions by his patients or on the difficulties that the families struggled with.

As February turned into March he began to notice the days lengthening. The new spring, he said to himself. Some of the bushes in the garden at the clinic were beginning to break into early leaf. For the first time since his mother's death he felt that he was beginning to notice what was around him. He felt less tearful; less often in the state of mind where memories of his mother would overwhelm him at moments of leisure in his flat. Perhaps it wasn't surprising that he began to notice the soprano in front of him at the choir practices, and he responded positively when she chatted enthusiastically during the tea break about the piece they were singing. He found himself responding warmly, even asking her if she would like to come for a walk in the countryside at the weekend. She accepted and on Saturday afternoon he found himself, almost without consciously willing it, having a lively conversation with Rachel as they walked through the early spring sunshine across the grass. She drew his attention to a magnolia tree putting up waxy white and pink blooms, sudden flourishes from the dark branches. He began to notice more of what was around him as she chatted and pointed out things of interest; the view of the distant city; a dog, a large Irish wolfhound, gaunt and grey, being led by an equally gaunt and grey old man.

He got into a routine of meeting Rachel at weekends, and eating with her before the choir, readily getting into a relationship. She was a lovely woman, although their interests, apart from music, did not coincide. She was a solace to him, understandably, he told himself. It was a serious relationship; but he could not feel about her as he felt about Clara. He felt guilty about what was, he felt, a trading on her good will. She was a kind, energetic, and cheerful person, talkative; she would speak at great length about her work, which involved something in the City. She was sleek; her straight blonde hair was shiny, and he liked the way it framed her rather long face. She looked the part for a City worker, sporting neat navy blue suits and crisp white blouses. Even her weekend clothes looked smart and her jeans were pressed. She lived in a wealthy London enclave, and her parents were rich, living in a large house in a Chilterns village. Her father commuted to his own job in the City. David could not help feeling that her parents regarded him with some suspicion—even incomprehension, puzzled by his work but to an extent impressed by it. They were less impressed by the obvious difference between the financial circumstances of their daughter and this new man in her life. He drove a car that had clearly seen better days, and his flat was modest.

Gradually, almost imperceptibly, David found himself involved in a relationship that he felt was enlivening, and that he enjoyed. He could not have Clara. He felt that he was lucky to have Rachel, who was attractive, and turned heads in the street. However, he could not feel that theirs was a relationship with a proper future, even when she abandoned her smart flat and moved into his. They had plans for holidays, and he found himself in the air at the beginning of his summer holiday, flying over the brown crinkled Alps en route for Corsica, which she had suggested as a suitable holiday destination. He was delighted with the break in his work, and looked down on the tiny island as it came into view with pleasure. The island looked like a toy from this height, sandy beaches golden at the edges of a deep-blue sea, and he thought, for a moment, it must be one of the islands off the south coast of France close to St Tropez that he had visited with his family as a teenager. He realised as the plane lost height that they were actually flying down to land at the tiny airport near Ajaccio. As they taxied to the small airport building he noticed that each telegraph pole was surmounted by a raven. He breathed in the hot Mediterranean air with pleasure, and felt that a holiday basking in the sun would restore him to a state approaching vitality. And it was pleasant to be there, even with a partner who talked almost incessantly; he remembered Jack saying of Rachel that she did not have a thought in her head but that it was voiced. They swam and snorkelled in the clear glassy-blue sea. They undertook a fishing trip, breathing in the warm breeze coming from the land, light zephyrs carrying the sweet smell of the maquis. The small boat seemed to be caressed, buoyed up by the slow heaves of the mirror-like sea. The heat and brightness of the light made them glad of the awning, and David felt that he was coming to life again after an intolerable age of darkness and blank despair. He was glad of his lively companion as they ate bowls of rich *soupe de poisson* in the restaurants or enjoyed siestas on hot sunny afternoons with the baked earth outside emitting a dry southern fragrance.

He found himself reminded of a visual fragment of the Joseph Losey film of *Don Giovanni*. Donna Anna, grieving for her father murdered by the Don, has drawn aside dark curtains in a palatial room, letting in the light, a visual comment on the change in her internal world as she begins to emerge from her devastating grief. What David did not comment on to himself, however, was his own role in his drama: he was conducting a relationship with someone, making her think there was a future for them together, whereas in fact it was simply his intense grief and need for distraction that drove him into her arms. He wondered if he was himself acting like a Don Giovanni figure, seducing a young woman with his attentiveness while ultimately having no real interest in her. Despite his best efforts his thoughts kept turning to Clara, wishing that she were there, not Rachel. He tried to turn a blind eye to his sense that the relationship with Rachel was a solution to the difficulty of moving on with his life, away from his grief, his disappointment about the Radcliffe's verdict, and away from his conviction that Clara, too, was lost to him.

## SEVEN

Back in London, David considered his position. He started work again with his patients and the families he saw at the clinic. The choir rehearsals were more enjoyable now that he had Rachel to compare notes with. Perhaps it was time to move forward, to reapply to the Radcliffe. He knew that it was possible to carry on applying. Nothing against that. This would be his second application, but when he wrote requesting a new application form he was disconcerted to receive a curt note back telling him he could not reapply. Puzzled, he wrote back and received another dismissive note telling him that, on the basis of his previous set of interviews, it was not felt appropriate to offer him another chance to apply.

He described this situation to Sonya, and was disconcerted when her response was to say, "Well, maybe they have picked up something about you. Maybe there's some anxiety about you? After all, you told me you felt down when your mother died, and you have actually been feeling quite depressed." She didn't link this loss with his infant experience of losing a warm maternal presence as a result of his overwhelming prematurity; the mark this had left. David knew that she didn't privilege infant experience in her thinking. He was stung into remarking that he felt that if most people didn't find themselves being depressed, and being very low, mourning, in the face of losing a parent, there might be something wrong with them … after all, Melanie Klein had famously written a paper about a similar bereavement reaction to the loss of her son, although ostensibly about someone else—and even Freud talked about the possible severity of mourning. Of course it was pointless to argue, and Sonya simply remarked that he seemed to want to minimise the seriousness of his psychological state. David left the session nettled, feeling once again that he was not in the presence of someone who had a compassionate understanding, based on her own struggles, of psychological issues, but someone who had a tick-box reaction to certain matters—even, said David to himself, a wilfully blind approach to the difficulties of her patient, someone who seemed to want to lodge her difficulties in the patient and criticise them there … and then he sighed and told himself that this was simply a parody of something Sonya had said to him earlier in the therapy about lodging his difficulties in his patients and looking after them there … for the first time, though, David began to think about ending this therapy, and finding another therapist who could think about his interior reality in a more cogent, understanding, and benign way. He wouldn't want to be the sort of psychotherapist Sonya was. No doubt she was helpful to patients who had not suffered early infantile trauma. He knew she had a good reputation, presumably because she helped patients whose internal reality didn't have its foundation in insecure and profoundly difficult early experience. Those patients did not need the sort of approach favoured by therapists who focused more actively on the way that early experience permeated emotional life. The more superficial stance of someone like Sonya would be appropriate for patients whose emotional reality had been forged in a secure early attachment.

More than a little angry at the Radcliffe's response to his application, David sent back a letter saying that at his follow-up interview he had been told by Paul French that he could reapply, and a time lapse of two years would be appropriate. He was then sent a new application form (in a grudging way, he thought angrily to himself) and he filled it in, wrote a statement about his current situation, and sent it back. Some three months later he was presenting himself again for a first interview with one of the therapists.

This interviewer was an extremely elderly man who sat bird-like on his chair, seeming so elderly as to be almost disabled. Andrew Highsmith had a kindly sociable manner. He was shocked to hear of David's bereavement, and was concerned enough to enquire whether he would not rather have deferred this set of interviews. David said that he saw no benefit in putting the application on hold, and that he was keen to move on as best he could with his professional development. David then had a very odd conversation with him, in which the therapist could not seem to grasp the specific details of what he was telling him about his early family life. David checked with him that he had understood a particular issue, and then told him that his view wasn't quite right, that it was as David had framed it. Andrew Highsmith seemed to bridle at this, and said perhaps it was David's imagination that he was making mistakes, through some idiosyncrasy. David considered this, but the issue was such a concrete one—whether he had one or two sisters. He must concede that Highsmith might be right, rather than challenge him.

He was beginning to realise Highsmith's cognitive ability might not be of the best. David did not want to insist, in case that jeopardised Highsmith's view of him; he feared that he might then go on to recommend that he shouldn't be accepted to train. He had the feeling all over again of watching an incompetent footballer scoring an own goal. The therapist was very pleasant in his manner, but David struggled with conveying detail that Highsmith found difficult to grasp. It was a bit like being with someone who had a good idea of what it was to function in a clinical setting, and was applying this as a formula, rather than someone who was engaging with him in a clear and coherent way.

David did not feel properly understood by Highsmith, who, he thought, seemed a little vague. When the therapist enquired about the difficulties of his university days David felt despair again as he realised that Highsmith was going to deal with it in a similar way to his previous interviewers. He went into clinician mode immediately and commented that David must have been very low as a student if he had crashed his car as he had done. David felt it would be impolitic now to take issue with him in case he accused him again of idiosyncrasy. He simply remarked that he had been able to move on successfully from that particular time in his life, which was associated with early prematurity, the struggle to establish himself, and to process feelings associated with the traumatic loss of his father.

As he left the interview he considered the way it had gone and he felt his heart sink. He felt as though he had been through yet another clinical interview where the point at issue was his psychological state of fifteen years ago. As though time had not passed. And in this interview he felt that it was worse than before, in that the therapist was so clearly elderly and forgetful, a bit muddled in his thinking. He did not feel that he had been with someone whose cognitive capacity was impressive. He sat in his car and groaned aloud, so much so that a passer-by walking a smart little black dog looked at him with curiosity. He realised that throughout the interview he had felt pressure to go along with Highsmith's view—he had not felt able to insist on his thought that Highsmith was in actuality making mistakes, or to argue with his rather negative view of him.

He recovered himself and, sitting over a quick lunch at his desk at work, rang Rachel and tried to explain his qualms to her. As usual, she found it as difficult to understand his experience with this issue as he did to understand the economic nuances of her work with the bank. Brightly she told him not to worry, she had picked up some of his favourite taramasalata for supper. And it seemed to him, later that afternoon in his session with Sonya, that he was even less understood. Her stance towards his interview was that the therapist must have been right to pick up his idiosyncrasy. It wasn't that he'd actually been making mistakes in his understanding of what David was saying, surely? It must have been that David easily felt misunderstood. Silently, David took issue with his therapist yet again. How was it that this woman could not seem to be on his wavelength? Was it his own problem? Was he transferring his early experience of life on to Sonya in a classic way?

As he considered the situation, he realised that in fact Sonya's stance might be an example of her closing ranks, wanting to protect her elderly colleague. Sonya had a senior role at the Radcliffe and would naturally side with her colleague. This thought seemed to lift some of David's mood. Perhaps this was an organisational issue. Sonya could not see the interview from his point of view. She actually needed to take a stance alongside colleagues. The Radcliffe was necessary to her: it provided her professional context; it was the pond in which she was a big fish. Not only that, but she needed to be protective of the interests of the Radcliffe, as it was the agency which provided her with work, the patients, through the network of contacts it embedded her in. David's thoughts surprised him. This was certainly a situation in which there was an organisational dimension. He needed to be careful of his idealisation of the place. It was quite problematic, if not difficult. And the fact of the matter was that it was his own professional development at issue; there was what felt like quite an obstruction to it emerging from clinicians at the Radcliffe. He mused on the way he had been dealt with, the attempts to put him off applying, and the way he had been spoken to so far in interviews. He had to admit to himself that he had over-idealised the place—and that his experience did not warrant such a level of positive regard. He must be careful not to denigrate, but he felt that he should go into the next interview cautiously, with his eyes open. And, he told himself, not transferring on to the institution feelings which might well belong to his early history.

Two weeks later he went to his second interview, this time with a slightly less elderly man, who was grey-haired and rather elegant in his dress. The same elegance permeated the house and his consulting room, which was in an expensive area. Michael Letchworth was affable. He said hello in an ordinary way, and seemed to be relating to David without any studied therapeutic cool or neutrality and he found this refreshing after the various experiences he had already had. However, like the others, Michael Letchworth took an interest in David's father's suicide and in David's difficulties as a student. David remarked that having had this experience he felt that he was likely to have more depth as a clinician.

"Oh, I don't think so," said Michael Letchworth pleasantly, as though he were not, in fact, saying something negative. "I don't think that having difficulties of one's own necessarily makes for greater capacity as a clinician ... Tell me, how old were you when you first had sex?"

Surprised, David told him—and this too was met with a negative response:

"Oh, that was a bit old, wasn't it?" As it happened, David did not think that his first sexual experiences were a suitable subject for an interview for a professional training; equally, he was willing to divulge frankly his first experiences if that was what his interviewer wanted, and he spent some time discussing his early sexual experiences in what he hoped was a self-reflective way.

When he told Rachel what he had been asked, and the interviewer's responses, she was surprised, even amused, and suggested what he himself thought, that this was an intrusive line of questioning to no very clear end. As she sipped her wine while they lingered over their supper discussing the day's events, she looked uneasy.

"David, are you sure that you want to be part of the Radcliffe? I mean, the interviews that you've had so far haven't been very impressive ..." Testily, he shrugged off her view and turned the conversation to something else.

The topic of conversation between them that led to most disagreement was whether or not they should get married and start a family. David felt under pressure on this issue: he wasn't sure that he was with the right partner and he certainly didn't want to go off down the track of starting a family with this issue unresolved. He wasn't sure whether it was something that could be resolved satisfactorily. He was sympathetic to Rachel's wish to have children before it was too late; but he did hesitate. They had been together for some years now but he was realising he did not want to stay with her long-term. There were long discussions. He was tuned into her reality in a compassionate way, and found it difficult to formulate thoughts about how to move things on between them in a way that did justice to each of their needs.

When he thought about his motivation, David wondered whether his family history made him reluctant to make the move into starting a family. He was dubious about fatherhood, having seen his own father struggle with the role as well as with his state of mind. David was still raw from the loss of his mother—and he was focused on taking on an extremely demanding training.

"You see, Rachel," he said one morning some weeks later as they had a trip out to the country valley where they often walked, "the difficulty is that if I got accepted to train, it would mean that I could easily be doing seventeen hours a week of training—unpaid."

She didn't seem to be concentrating on what he was saying, peering up the hillside towards a herd of cows grazing peacefully some way off. Their path lay along the bottom of the valley, beside a clear chalk river. Moorhens dabbled in the water. Autumn colour seemed poised to take over from the heavy green of the summer foliage. On the far bank a solitary egret pleated its wings.

"I wonder if there's any spindle-berry out yet," she said, scanning the bushes at the end of the field where the woodland took over.

"You're not listening to me, Rachel!" David protested with a slight edge to his tone as he hefted the weight of the rucksack on his shoulder.

"Yes I am!" She smiled warmly at him, the low sun picking out golden feathers of light in her blonde hair. "You were saying it would be seventeen hours of work a week if you did the training. So who's going to pay for that, then?" He was surprised again at her capacity to appear to be thinking of something else but actually to be listening to him; he thought often and uncharitably that she had an airy mentality, floating through life with unconcern and a lack of serious focus. Once again he remarked to himself that, even so, she had enough focus to get herself the job in the city …

"Well, I will, of course," he said shortly. "My mother left me some money, as you know."

She frowned. Not happy, he could see. Whenever they discussed plans for the future, they came up against this obstacle: she wanted children, he wanted to pursue his career.

"Oh, God!" she said irritably. "Of course you will. So why are you raising the seventeen hours as an issue, then?"

"I was just thinking aloud. Thinking about what it would mean time-wise if I had two training patients three times a week each that I was seeing for the training, and then a weekly supervision for each, then my own therapy, then the clinical discussion group, then in addition to that, the reading and the theoretical seminar …"

"Wouldn't you rather just stay as you are and have a baby … if we had a baby, we'd need to move house, of course, we'd need the space …"—her voice trailed off as she saw the obdurate look on his face. "Well here we are again," she said with a harsh, disappointed tone. "Been here before, haven't we?"

"Oh, come on, Rachel, it's a lovely day, let's not argue." David took her hand as they walked down a little slope to the bank of the river. There was a metal bridge over it, with a gate bearing a sign saying it was placed there in memory of someone. "Life's too short to make each other miserable," he said as they paused in the middle of the bridge, looking down into the water and seeing the shapes of trout flicking their tails and holding their positions against the current. On the far side of the bridge he could see that the river bank had been partly washed away and there was a considerable stream rushing down into the marshy area beyond.

"Look, you can see where there's been a bit of a flood," he said to change the subject and they looked at the stream rushing through the gap in the bank.

"Needs fixing, that," she said. "Come on, let's walk on the other side of the river—and look, there are some blackberries. I'd like to pick some, I could make some blackberry crumble. No sign of the spindle-berry that was here last year. You going to help me pick some?"

"No, if you don't mind I'll just walk on and round the top of the hill to get some exercise. You come back to the car when you're ready."

He left her to her foraging and walked on, not really noticing the bright orange and red hips in the hedgerows or the glistening purple spangles of the elderberry. He was lost in the puzzle of how to make it possible for them both to move in the direction they wanted to. It was like a three-legged race, he said to himself—but they wanted to go in different directions just now.

Back at the car, he waited for what seemed an interminable time for Rachel to reappear and, when she did, she came from the hillside, looking tired and clearly having walked further than she had intended to.

"What happened to you?" he asked. "You've been a very long time. I was thinking of going to look for you."

"That herd of cows—they had a bull with them—and some bullocks—they all came trotting down the hill towards me—I didn't notice them, I was picking blackberries—I just had time to get into the wood through the gate."

"You need to be careful of cows with young ones," he said, looking at her with some concern.

"I'm fine, just a bit tired now, that's all," she said. "Any coffee left? It was just a bit scary, there was one cow in the lead, positively aiming straight for me, making eye contact—I had to move sharpish to get out of the way."

"Glad you *did* move fast," he said, handing her the flask of coffee. "I don't want to make any jokes, but didn't Ariadne give Theseus a thread that showed the way to escape the Minotaur? You clearly didn't have your thread with you today."

To his relief she smiled, even laughed a little. Perhaps the difficulty of their conversation could be left behind and he could manage tea with her parents in their garden, with the thought that the conflict between them had, if only temporarily, been laid aside.

# EIGHT

David got a letter from the Radcliffe in January. He had been turned down again. He was disappointed, even though he had come to expect this sort of response. That evening they were going out with Jack and his partner Marie; they had tea together at a concert hall where they were going to hear a celebrated tenor give a recital of Schubert Lieder with a distinguished pianist as accompanist. Jack was startled to hear the news that David had been turned down.

"They don't know what's good for them," he said gruffly and then added: "If you were someone foreign—if you had a Russian accent—or better still a Lithuanian one—or if you were from Latin America—you would've been accepted …" Rachel looked at him, puzzled.

"Why's that?" she asked. "Are they more in favour of you if you're foreign?"

"He's just joking," said David uncomfortably. But as the concert began he did begin to find himself wondering if there was perhaps some truth in what Jack had said. Would he have been more in favour if he were not so clearly and identifiably an ordinary person from the UK? Albeit with a Swiss father?

He shrugged and left the thought as he focused on the Lieder. The singer had a delicately nuanced voice, a voice which had dark undertones with some warmth in the quiet passages but which was bright and forceful in the loud. He wished his tenor voice had the same lyrical vibrancy. He was singing a favourite of David's—"*Viola*"—which starts off as an address to a *Schneeglöcklein*, a snowdrop, and turns into a lament for a violet; it has bloomed too early, so that when, in its loneliness it is sought, at the behest of the *Schneeglöcklein*, by the other flowers that come out in the spring, it has already perished in the cold. The tune of the first few lines, which returns again and again through the piece has a sweet lilting tone that speaks of desolation, early bloom, and promise lost. David found himself thinking about Schubert; about his early death and the sadness of his life, which found such piercingly painful expression. The song carried a weight of meaning that David leant on, psychically, finding an immediacy in it that spoke to the disappointment burdening him at that moment, but also to the unbearable poignancy of existing, minute by minute. It was cathartic, he decided.

In the interval they drank wine and talked. Despite being jostled by groups of people, Marie seemed disposed to talk of intimate matters and, clearly unable to manage to contain herself any longer, told David and Rachel that she and Jack were expecting a baby. Amidst congratulations, David could see that Rachel was upset and, sure enough, once home from the concert she became disconsolate and bitter about his reluctance to start a family. He avoided a lengthy conversation with her by pleading tiredness and the fact that he was getting up early the next day to go for a run with Jack.

Broaching the subject with Jack as they trotted through the early mist next day, he was interested to hear that Jack was not surprised that he had reservations about starting a family with Rachel.

"I always did wonder a bit whether you're suited" he said hesitantly. David was momentarily disposed to bluff, to pretend that all was well with Rachel, and that he just wasn't ready to think of having a family. He decided to be straightforward, and found that actually it was a relief to talk through his doubts about his relationship with Rachel.

"She's a lovely person, Jack … but we don't seem to have enough in the way of shared interests, if you know what I mean." Jack did know what he meant, which was a comfort but it still left him with a problem; Rachel was increasingly unhappy with him as his concerns and hers diverged. He could not commit himself to her, doubting, as he did, the viability of their relationship. And it seemed unfair to her, to keep up the relationship if he actually felt they had no future together. It was a relief to discuss all this with Jack who listened thoughtfully to what he had to say, and could even confide his ambivalence about his own circumstances: the pregnancy; Marie's views on it; his worries about managing the training at the Radcliffe with its demands on his time; and his need to earn money to keep them both, whilst also coping with new parenthood.

"Not easy," said David. As they ran down the muddy gravelled path, as though to provide a backdrop to their anxieties the heavy cloud above them began to release a fine snowfall, the flakes getting larger as they approached the grey choppy waters of the lake. The snow was soon so heavy that it was difficult to see across the lake to the hill opposite with its delicate tracings of tree branches black against the tawny colour of the grass. The path quickly lost its definition as the snow turned it white, and there was a slipperiness underfoot that made them slow down cautiously.

"Not easy running conditions either," David continued, and they cut their run short, angling back up the hill towards their cars. They arranged a meeting for lunch later in the week, and parted, David returning with some reluctance to Rachel.

Her mood seemed to have shifted, the sight of the snow pleasing her. Not for the first time, he was relieved at the natural buoyancy that seemed to tide her over the difficult moments.

David was undecided what to do; confiding his doubts to Sonya, it was clear that she felt negatively about his stance in relation to Rachel. Once again, David felt that he had a therapist who was going to find fault with him, and this was now unendurable. The combination of her comments and apparent reluctance to support the application to the Radcliffe was very difficult, and again, on a run the following weekend, David talked to Jack about his experience. Jack was uncharacteristically bombastic.

"Well, it's not very analytic to be taking sides with Rachel— obviously so—is it?" he asked David. David considered this. When he thought about it, he felt that it wasn't. It was a comment on a real relationship in his life rather than sticking to the task of the psychotherapist as he saw it, which was to comment on the unfolding of the transference, the early relationships which were actualised in the consulting room.

"It's not—no, you're right, Jack," he said. "Does your therapist comment on these sorts of things?" The answer, of course, was a negative one; Jack had originally had the good sense to go to a psychotherapist who belonged to the Dr Smythe set. Such therapists were sought after, and it was fortunate for Jack to have been accepted by the Radcliffe. This had given him access to the well-thought-of therapists. David said something of this to Jack.

"Yes, you're in a difficult situation," Jack acknowledged, as they stopped breathless at the top of the rise looking out over the city. The new many-storied buildings rose jagged and tall from the distant landscape like crystals growing organically from a Petri dish. The mist had cleared and the still cold air was now sunlit. The snow on the grass was sparkling in the brightness.

"Perhaps ..."

"Yes?"

"Well, I wonder if it would reflect badly on me if I changed to a different therapist."

"Reflect badly with whom, David? You're the one who needs to make the choice ..."

"Yes, I know. It's just that Sonya is a training psychotherapist and ... I want to apply again to the Radcliffe—having a training therapist makes it more likely that I'd be accepted, of course. Would it look bad if I had changed to someone else?"

"I see what you mean. You're certainly persistent. I know you can apply again, but ..." Jack considered the question. Slowly he said, "Would you consider applying again, without being in therapy? The only way you are going to get a training psychotherapist from the Spaltung set is by being accepted ..."

"Spaltung?" queried David. He could see the droplets of the early mist melting and gleaming on the branches of bushes nearby. Jack's gaze lingered on the far view.

"Well, you know, that's Freud's term for splitting, and the set that Dr Smythe belonged to, and which Sonya doesn't belong to, is called the Spaltung set. That's because it has that particular theoretical viewpoint about the early split view of his mother the infant goes in for. Both good and bad, loved and hated. They value making sense of infantile experience, how early experience has a formative effect on the internal world." David knew the term, familiar as he was with the technical considerations of the psychotherapeutic task in his counselling practice. But he hadn't heard before what this set of therapists called themselves, and the fact that he didn't know, and that Jack did, made him feel very excluded.

"Oh, I see. Yes ... perhaps that's the best way forward. I just feel with Sonya that there isn't a good match—I think I'm the wrong patient for her. And she's certainly the wrong psychotherapist for me."

"Yes … you could end the therapy with her on that basis. I don't think that anyone interviewing would necessarily think badly of you if you explained the situation. Everyone knows that there is such a thing as a good fit between patient and psychotherapist. And of course, if you stayed with her and did train, you would find yourself belonging to her set."

David felt relieved. He thought he could see the way forward. He would end with Sonya. Why should he pay money to be criticised in this endless way? He felt he was always in the wrong in the therapy. However Sonya might wrap it up by being personally pleasant, he did not feel that he could continue.

"Thanks, Jack," he said as they went their separate ways at the end of the run. "I think I'm a bit clearer about the best way forward." He felt contrite at having used their conversation so much to air his concerns, and returned to the fact that Jack was expecting their first baby, congratulating him warmly. Jack beamed.

"I am excited," he said. "But it's the financial stuff that's so difficult." David found this difficult to imagine since Jack came from a wealthy family and was a medic, but he knew that he worked long hours at the clinic, as did Marie. He said something suitably supportive and headed back towards his flat where Rachel was taking advantage of his absence by getting on with some work she had brought home for the weekend. Relieved as he was at the prospect of ending the psychotherapy with Sonya and seeing a clearer way forward, David felt sympathetically disposed towards her, and by dint of avoiding the contentious subject they contrived to spend the Sunday afternoon in a pleasant way.

The next day he approached his session with Sonya with a sense of foreboding, if not anxiety. Sonya was surprised when David told her of his intention to leave. David was hard put to it to agree to a month's notice. Sonya tried to persuade him to make it a longer lead-in time to the end, but David felt he could no longer tolerate the stance of his pleasant but unendingly critical therapist. As he left the session, he tangled as usual with the next patient who always arrived early and spent some time outside chaining up his bike to the railings and unclipping his bicycle clips—and was probably already training at the Radcliffe, remarked David bitterly to himself. He said hello, but felt himself snarl unpleasantly.

Surprisingly, David's sense of relief far outweighed any negative feelings he had in relation to ending the therapy. He could shrug off Sonya's view that he was passing on the disappointment of being rejected by the Radcliffe to her, by deciding unilaterally, without discussion, to end. He could even shrug off another comment from Sonya, in which she meditated aloud on the possibility that David was replaying the sudden loss of his father by ending precipitately. David thought to himself that of course Sonya would carry on interpreting right to the end, but that she would never consider thoughtfully the sorts of criticisms that David was making of her therapeutic stance.

And that was in fact exactly what happened. In the final session it was more comment about what it was that David was doing wrong, in wanting to end the therapy. At the end, Sonya's line—"It's time to stop for today"—made David feel unable to say anything other than to comment on the fact that it was time to stop for ever, not just for today. Sonya smiled and David felt again that whatever he said would not be understood and carefully thought about; it was water off a duck's back. Perhaps Sonya was glad he was going.

David found the next few months depressing. He was doubtful about his relationship with Rachel and he was, of course, doubtful about the direction of his career. It was difficult to sustain a sense of momentum, of things moving on for himself.

The winter dragged on in a cold and interminable way. The gloom of the early spring seemed to be endless, accentuating his state of mind; a miasma of greyness seemed to descend, much as he struggled to keep his work active and to work creatively with the patients and families he saw. He began to worry that they were also stuck, like their psychologist. The family in which Petra and Wilma struggled to separate filled him with despair about the possibility of progress. Much as he tried to think of his feelings about them as to do with their despair, he found it difficult to bear with the endless and rather concrete descriptions of daily life from Wilma. He found the stance of his co-therapist Simon helpful, however, along with the continual sense of lively discussion about clinical matters from the working group. But he began to feel he was lumbering through his days like some prehistoric creature, unable to shake off his disappointment in both the Radcliffe and his therapist.

It was during this phase that he began to feel that the work he was doing with Petra's mother, Wilma, was worrying. He could not speak for Simon's work with Petra, but there seemed little change. As he had predicted, the learning mentor who had been providing one-to-one support for Petra in school suddenly said that she felt she could not continue to offer this degree of support for one child. She needed to divide her time more equally among the students. There were others who were as deserving of help as Petra, surely? David set up a meeting with her and the head teacher in school, but got the same message. Apprehensively, he awaited the outcome of the meeting the learning mentor had arranged with Wilma. She told Wilma too that she could not offer the same degree of support to Petra. Wilma, like David, argued the case and tried her best to convey Petra's degree of need, but to no avail. David, despite his anxiety about Wilma undermining the attempts of her daughter to separate from her, was forced to conclude that Wilma had done her best. The day after the learning mentor support was withdrawn, Petra refused to attend school. Wilma, communicating this news to David, was full of criticism of the school.

When David considered the situation, he decided that perhaps the family dynamics had become lodged in the network. The network was made up of him, the head teacher, the learning mentor, and the child psychotherapist. It was unusual for a learning mentor to devote herself so completely to one student; it was very reminiscent of the way that Wilma devoted herself to Petra. The one mirrored the other. And the sudden way the arrangement broke down mirrored the unpredictable violence of the parental couple in Wilma's mind, and the sudden breakdown of Wilma's relationship with Petra's father. Also the sudden shock of Petra's serious illness as a baby, and the need to have intrusive and alarming surgery in a life-threatening situation. David could see the situation with the clarity of a general sitting on his horse on a hillside overlooking a battle down below. What he could not do was influence it for the better—unless he was able to discuss some of this with Simon and with Wilma. He hoped that if the scenario could be discussed with his co-worker and with Wilma they could function better as reinforcements in the battle to get the school to provide appropriate support for Petra. He smiled to himself as he remembered his Latin studies at school, the cavalry wing, the ala, being sent in to reinforce the legionaries in some epic battle. He decided to talk to Simon.

Knocking on Simon's door later that day at a time he knew he would be free, he realised that he had rarely sat in Simon's room discussing the work with him. This was what was needed. If they could work together creatively—as a sort of grand-parenting parental couple for Wilma and Petra—they might be able to help with the separation needed between them so that Petra could get on with the task of being a young adolescent separating from her mother. A separation of a benign sort, enabling her to attend school appropriately.

"Am I disturbing you, Simon?" he asked as he put his head round the door. Simon sat back from his computer and stretched.

"No, come in, David," he said. "You're only disturbing endless diary entries."

"Just wanted to have a word about Petra and Wilma," David said, sitting down firmly, with purpose, hoping to convey to Simon a clear need for them to discuss the situation. "Wilma told me just now when I saw her that Petra's refusing to go to school again. That's since the learning mentor said she wasn't going to devote her time exclusively to her anymore."

"Oh, God," said Simon, raising his eyes heavenward. "What possessed the mentor to do that? Very unhelpful. If she was going to stop supporting Petra, she should have withdrawn gradually, in a graded way ..." He stood up suddenly, going to the window, looking down on the garden where a grape vine was putting out little pale green buds.

"Well, yes, absolutely," said David, talking to his back. "I did talk to the head teacher and the learning mentor about this, and they simply went on about the other children needing help too. Maybe the dynamics in the family are reflected in the sudden decision they made."

Simon's face looked even more lined and squashed than normal. His hair had been cut shorter and this accentuated its bristling slightly aggressive appearance, which was at such odds with his mild manner and softness of speech. He turned round and sat down again.

"That's true enough, but Petra's a special case. She really needs the support to get back into school properly."

"I agree, Simon," said David. He described to Simon, as well as he could, his thinking about the dynamics of the case, the way that the sudden withdrawal of support mirrored the family dynamics of violence, sudden illness, and sudden departures. Simon ran his hand over his hair in an effort to get it to lie down, looking thoughtful. For the first time David felt that he was with a colleague who was in a proper working relationship with him, rather than a colleague who was fending him off while desperately trying to keep afloat in a sea of overwork.

"Well, look, David, I do think what you're saying is very interesting. I do think it's accurate, in fact. But how are we going to make use of this understanding in our work with the family?"

"The first idea I have, the one that comes to mind initially, is that it might be helpful for us to have regular discussions about our joint work, to work together more, so that we can be a creative working partnership. You know how Wilma's a single parent, there's no actual creative parental couple either in her mind, or in reality, since Petra's father isn't available … If we work more closely together, share our thinking, we're constituting a joint thinking partnership which could be quite helpful. I don't know if it would make a difference but it may do. The other thought I have is that perhaps we should get an educational psychologist involved, who could work with the school constructively in the interests of getting Petra back there. I think in the head teacher's mind I'm too linked with Wilma. I think she feels I'm too soft and sympathetic … school have felt about Wilma for a long time that she allows Petra to stay off for the slightest cough and cold … and of course Wilma thinks they are quite unsympathetic. An educational psychologist bridging the gaps between the school and home, and school and the clinicians, might be very useful."

"Yes. I agree with you on both counts. I can see the benefit of us working more closely together. I can also see the benefit of involving one of the ed psychs. Let me see. Who's the ed psych for the school?" He consulted a list on his computer.

"It's Raymond. He's impressive, very thoughtful and very much liked by the school."

"What do you think, shall we have a meeting with Raymond so we can fill in the picture for him?"

Simon thought this a good idea. They compared diaries, and rang Raymond, who worked in a different building on the other side of the borough. He was able to take on the work and sounded interested. They met, and he agreed to take on the liaison work with the school. Under pressure from him, the head teacher agreed to apply for more funding to provide more support for Petra.

David began to feel a little more hopeful as this work started to move forward again. His private practice as a counsellor, which was not subject to the overload strain of his NHS work, began to feel a little less draining. He realised that the spring was generally a good time of year for him, and despite the difficulty with Rachel, their relationship seemed to settle down.

He began to look around for another job in the NHS. Financial constraints in the public sector meant that there were few posts available and it was the autumn again before he noticed one coming up. It would be a difficult journey for him, as they were living a distance away, but he thought it would be worth applying in order to get a more senior post where he would be supervising students. He applied, was shortlisted, but at the interview was concerned when he was asked how he dealt with difficult organisational dynamics. He answered promptly in a concrete fashion that he simply focused as best he could on the clinical work. He thought of asking whether there were difficult dynamics in the clinical team but felt this would be inappropriate and might lose him the job. The team was well-founded in terms of the numbers of clinical staff able to undertake the work: there were many child psychotherapists, two consultant child psychiatrists, and a clinical psychologist. Again, his job very specifically entailed work with the parents of the children seen by the child psychotherapists, and he sensed in the interview that his psychoanalytic stance was a welcome one in relation to the child psychotherapists.

There was another clinical psychologist whom he knew from his clinical psychology training, and the building was a pleasant one, a modern clinic with many spacious rooms so that he would be able to have an office of his own, which would double as the room in which he saw families and parents. There was a good-sized room that served as meeting room, staff-room, and library. To the rear was a pleasant garden, nicely kept up with a few interesting trees. He would be sad to leave his existing job, enjoying as he did the lively case discussions and the cosy setting in a lovely area close to where he lived. There would be some colleagues whom he would continue to see, however, and that alleviated the difficulty of leaving.

He was pleased to be offered the post. Predictably, his departure from his existing post entailed some careful reviewing of his caseload, ending with some families, transferring others to colleagues. He was sorry to be stopping the work with Wilma and Petra, but progress there was solid, with Petra having started the new school year in a positive way and her mother beginning to look around for work possibilities. The separation issues were becoming less of an issue. There was a period of difficulty when he had to give Wilma the news that he was leaving, but the work with her was going to be undertaken by a child psychotherapist colleague whom he was able to brief, and he felt reasonably confident that the new period of work after he had gone would continue well.

It took until Christmas to work out his notice. He went out for the Christmas dinner with his colleagues with a comfortable sense that he was leaving a job that he had made a success of, and in which he had made a good contribution. Whatever faced him in his new post must build on the work he had done already. He and Rachel went to hear *Messiah* and he felt his mood lifting in line with the powerful singing of the choir who performed the familiar piece with a profound depth and precision. He wished their choir could command such a presence and capacity. On Christmas Day he went with Rachel to her parents for Christmas dinner, along with her brother and his wife and small children. The children provided a welcome distraction from the rigours of the occasion in the slightly heavy atmosphere at Rachel's home. Her mother was a lively enough woman, but her father created an atmosphere of tension, given as he was to negative comment about any subject. David was tired of his apparent determination to take the high ground on each issue. No subject could be raised but that he would lift his delicately arched eyebrows and deliver a definitive view that brooked no argument. David had no interest in golf? *Everybody* liked golf. David felt that the government in power was having a devastating effect on the public sector? *Far* more competent than the previous government. David skittered nervously away from the possibility of a discussion about politics, which he knew would have him and Rachel's father at odds almost immediately. He turned to Rachel's mother and complimented her on the food she had prepared. For him this was a particular issue, as he was a long-standing vegetarian and his plate of food showed the care and thoughtfulness she had devoted to it. And it was a short hop from there to turn the conversation again to the children.

Rachel managed not to look too saddened at the fact that her brother had two lively children whilst she was still trying to persuade David of the timeliness of their starting a family too. Her brother looked harassed—his wife wasn't much better— and David took a turn with entertaining the children as the dinner progressed, enjoying playing with them as they had fun with their new toys. He picked up a grateful glance from the beleaguered parents, and when they all tumbled out after lunch for a walk in the early dusk of the winter evening he was reasonably cheerful. He and Rachel were going on to have tea with his stepfather Evan and his children. David's two sisters Jay and Susie and their partners would be there. It was a useful pretext to make his escape.

Evan was struggling after the death of David's mother. He was making an effort to get over the terrible loss to play host to his children on Christmas Day, and with David and his two sisters there for tea. To David's eye the photograph of his mother looking down on them all from a shelf as they gathered in Evan's living room was a mute reminder of their painful loss. He had to will himself to turn his attention to the various conversations required with each of those gathered over the Christmas cake. Shop-bought, he noticed, not his mother's light fruitcake topped with brandied marzipan. Evan's two children were teenagers now, two boys who were surprisingly forthcoming when David chatted to them about their interests. His sisters had their partners with them.

The eldest of his two sisters, Jay, was an academic, married to another lecturer, Sam, and he felt it would not be long before they had a family. They struggled to manage financially despite two salaries, working long hours at their respective universities in order to afford their little flat in a fashionable area. Jay was a bright and outgoing woman, and Sam was equally lively, a handsome man with light brown hair over a high brow and bright blue eyes. David could not but imagine that they were very successful in their work and that their young students benefitted enormously from their liveliness and charm, exhausted charm though it was by the end of every week. His youngest sister, Susie, was quieter and wore her blonde hair in a modish straight cut, short at the back with dangling earrings. She and her stonemason partner were both scraping a living doing some teaching and living in a community house in East London. Both wore clothes that had clearly seen better days but which were artistically matched to convey an impressive sense of style.

It was an animated gathering—academic and artistic—and he could see Rachel, who was dressed in an expensive dress and heels and wearing gold earrings, beginning to flounder. She was a lively person, however, and David felt it was a generous impulse that led her to engage Evan in a lengthy conversation about his work situation at the university where he taught German. He was an enthusiast, and it wasn't long before he was deep in the intricacies of departmental politics and Rachel listened politely, making, David felt, a good effort at showing real interest. He knew that if she attempted to talk to Evan about the politics at the bank he would struggle far more to be attentive, politically biased as he was against the morality of the big banks and by what he thought of as an extractive economy run for the benefit of the already wealthy.

# NINE

A few days later David started work in the new child and adolescent consultation service. He was welcomed by all the staff at a team meeting—when asked about his orientation there were nods of satisfaction when he said that his theoretical interests clinically encompassed both systemic and psychoanalytic approaches. He was surprised and gratified at the number of child psychotherapists, and took a keen interest in the clinical presentation that formed part of the meeting. He noticed that the child psychiatrist, Thea, was quite active, and dominant in the discussion. She was a large woman, with light brown hair and a pleasant manner, and a voice that was quiet but nonetheless cut through the vagaries of the discussion like a knife through butter. He thought her comments apposite and interesting. The principal child psychotherapist was also a woman, but a different type altogether, slightly vague, withdrawn, and with an anxious look. Frieda's contribution to the discussion was careful and limited to one comment. His impression of her as rather withdrawn was underlined when he noticed that she made no real attempt to engage with him over the next few weeks. He found his other child psychotherapy colleagues and the other clinical psychologist more willing to get to know him and he was grateful for the time they gave to welcoming him, despite the endemic NHS work overload.

Gradually his mood began to lift under the influence of his new work setting and the sense he had there that he was welcome and his input valued. His counselling practice was going well too; he felt that the work with the patients was beginning to be meaningful again and he had a new supervisor for the work whose thoughtful comments each week were very valuable, coming as she did from the Spaltung group of psychotherapists, which privileged early experience. He felt he was in sympathy with her approach.

David had a consulting room on the second floor of an Edwardian house, in a house owned by an entrepreneurial landlord who knew that consulting rooms were needed, and who had furnished the house in a pleasant neutral manner, renting out rooms to a selection of psychotherapists and counsellors. David's room was at the back of the house, very quiet and away from the traffic noise at the front. It had a marble fireplace on which stood a gilt-framed mirror and plants. The couch was covered with a woollen checked rug, the chairs antique and comfortable. The desk stood in the window so that David could sit at it looking down at the garden. In winter, side lamps provided a warm glow and in summer the sunshine flooded the room with light, so much so that on hot afternoons David needed to pull the curtains across as well as lower the slatted blinds. David was attached to the room and felt that it provided a supportive but muted setting in which he could allow his mind to roam free and uninterrupted as he attended to the thoughts brought by his patients.

When one patient, Hugh, seemed to value the work so highly that he wanted to come to see him three times a week, David felt rewarded, and, although it would be difficult to fit into his working week, he felt that it was real progress; it would deepen the work, make it more substantial. Hugh was an unhappy man, twenty-eight, from a privileged background but with a history of neglect in his early life. The youngest of three brothers, his parents had separated when he was six and he had very little contact with his father after that. He was sent away to boarding school at the age of eight. He was chronically anxious and depressed. In the sessions he came across in a way that was determinedly normal, despite his rather odd look, one eye green, the other brown. His mother was Spanish, and his skin colour, which was a warm brown, contrasted strangely with his light brown hair. He had an easy smile and manner derived from his public school background, but the hunted look that occasionally overcame him belied his sociable manner.

Hugh had found the work in the psychodynamic counselling difficult to begin with; it was hard to go along with a stance from his counsellor that privileged his depressed and needy self, a self he would rather not acknowledge but which undermined him in his working life. He worked for a bank and found the autocratic style of his seniors there difficult; however, he found the routine expectations of the job provided him with a much-needed sense of structure and security, almost as though he were back in his school years. Depression had almost overwhelmed him when he had been made redundant in a previous job, this driving him to seek counselling, which now he was beginning to value and work well in.

One day when David had been in his new post for some months and the spring was beginning to make itself felt, Hugh arrived for his session uncharacteristically early. David felt it was going to be a useful session. Hugh looked eagerly from the waiting area as David invited him into his room. He looked tousled and said that he had rushed to get to the session as he'd had difficulty in sleeping the previous night and had woken late. It was the second session of his three sessions that week and David knew that characteristically he was more settled and in tune with the work of the counselling in the middle session of the week; he found the Monday session difficult, after what felt, to the more vulnerable part of him, like being abandoned by his counsellor over the weekend, and the Thursday session, the last of the week, difficult because of the impending weekend break. He often reported that his sleep had been disturbed by nightmares but rarely spoke of the content of the dreams. He would stick rigidly to reporting the daily routine in minute and rather obsessional detail, and dealt with David's interpretative comments by pausing in his relaying of detail and then going back to it. He didn't seem to acknowledge what David had said. He had begun to respond to the idea that his attention to detail was a way he had developed as a boy of dealing with his sense of his parents neglecting him, being caught up in their own desperation, and he had used this to hold himself together when sent to boarding school. He had begun to be able to pay attention to his internal life. His descriptions of the boarding school were vivid. When he described his first days there, he was very much in touch with the poignancy of the state of mind of the group of boys he was with, all struggling with their sense of isolation and secret homesickness.

One of the things he had enjoyed before leaving home for boarding school, and which he described often, was the succession of pets on which he and his brothers lavished care and attention. There was the family cat, a rather ordinary cat for so wealthy a family, which had joined them as a stray found on their doorstep. He described with pleasure the cat sleeping on his bed at night; and with equal pleasure the habits of the guinea-pig that one of his brothers owned. This little animal would be set to roam among the flower beds, as in a verdant jungle, and would fell tall lupins by crunching through the stems with great enthusiasm, much to the boys' delight and the gardener's fury.

In this session, Hugh laughed as he reported that he had dreamt the previous night, not a nightmare, but a dream about gulls—fancy that, he said, what an odd thing to dream about!

David held his breath momentarily. Was he going to tell the detail of the dream? It would be progress if he would go into detail; dreams reported by his other patients bore out and underlined Freud's description of them as being the royal road to the unconscious. To his amazement, Hugh gave a detailed account of the dream. He had been at the seaside with his family. There was bright sunshine. He and his brothers were going to swim. Just as they were going towards the water, a huge flock of seagulls appeared. They flew around their heads, and in his dream Hugh was filled with anxiety and despair as he knew, for some reason, that he would have to look after them— but there were so many, how could he? He asked his brothers to help him call all the birds in, like calling in chickens at night to their coop, but they laughed and ran away. His father and mother were there and he asked them to help too but they were busy talking to each other and hardly noticed him. He awoke in a panic.

"Quite a dream, don't you think?" he said. David paused. He needed time to think, to make sense of this dream.

"What do you make of it?" he asked, playing for time, pleased that Hugh had brought a dream but trying to decide how far to link it with Hugh's needy self which was so often deeply camouflaged.

"Well, I think it relates to what was happening at work yesterday," said Hugh and went into a detailed description of a meeting where he felt he had to take on the work of the moment, and look after his colleagues in doing so.

"Well, that's certainly one way of looking at it," said David. "We know that you do tend to take on work and look after others in doing so … taking on too much, exhausting yourself, trying to placate your bosses."

"Yes, that's it exactly," said Hugh. "I've got so much work on. I'm constantly doing overtime. No wonder I woke in a state of panic." David thought that this surface-level explanation of the dream's meaning was rather apposite, but ultimately would not take them further in the work of the counselling. Hugh was quite comfortable with this sort of description of his tendency to look after others and to become the office maid-of-all-work, even laughing at it. David decided to take matters further.

"We could look at it like that. However, I wonder if there's more to your dream than that. I wonder if it's actually about that side of you that we've talked about before. The side of you that came to the fore when you were sent off to boarding school. I wonder if you feel that, like with the seagulls, there would be too much for you to deal with in attending to the needy sides of yourself. You move away in panic from those dependent needy selves because you feel you risk being overwhelmed by them. They have to be sent away."

There was silence for a minute while Hugh digested this. In the silence, David could hear birds outside in the garden, sparrows cheeping in the spring warmth and a robin's wavering warble. In the building he heard the front door close as someone left the building.

"Maybe," said Hugh. He stopped, David resisted the temptation to push him. "Maybe I don't feel so much like sending that part of myself away any more," Hugh said.

"Exactly. You feel able to tell me the detail of the dream. You feel able to come to three sessions a week here in your counselling. You don't feel so inclined to push this part of yourself away. You bring it here for us to think about. Nevertheless, I wonder if your changing the number of sessions each week, so that you are coming to three not two, has made you feel anxious, and has sparked this dream that you've had. You're not sure whether I will be like your brothers or your parents, pushing your needs away."

David was relieved that he had been able to link the dream to Hugh's experience of the counselling; he felt, like the Spaltung set of therapists that he identified with, that he was able to work effectively in the transference, linking the material of the session to the patient's experience in the session, in the here and now of the relationship to the counsellor, in an effective way, whilst also referencing early experience. He thought that his supervisor would think well of him when he reported the detail of this session to her. Progress had been made. He waited with some interest to see whether Hugh would feel able to take in this comment, or whether he would brush it aside, not able to resist the temptation to turn his counsellor into the little boy sent away instead. To send him away rather than endure being sent away himself.

"Mmm—I think maybe you're right. I did feel pleased about coming to three sessions a week, but I also felt worried—could you possible stand seeing me three times a week?" He stopped and then went on. "Or would you want to send me away?" Laughing now, a free and light laugh. "Nasty raucous things, seagulls."

Thinking about this session later as he wrote his notes, sitting gazing down into the garden sparkling in spring sunshine, David permitted himself a moment of hopefulness and pleasure in the progress made by Hugh. This was real work, the sort of work he was committed to, and which he wanted to improve by training at the Radcliffe. He laughed to himself. Here we are again, he thought to himself. Well, the Radcliffe certainly sent me away. A fate suffered by many competent people. Why was that? Was his clinical capacity, his ability to work psychotherapeutically, very different from Jack's—or Clara's? And what would prove to them that he was as good? He laughed again. He wouldn't say better—that would be overweening—he would allow their capacity to be larger than his—after all, Jack was a medic—but surely he had something to offer? He began to wonder about his continuing sense of exclusion. With the Radcliffe, it was a little like a particular clan going inside a castle, pulling up the drawbridge—excluding themselves from participation in ordinary life, with no real links, for example to the NHS. But could it be that they reversed the whole thing, so that people who wanted to train there, but who were often barred, were left with this sense of exclusion themselves. He wondered about it from an organisational point of view. Could it be that Freud started this dynamic off? His own sense of exclusion as a Jew in Vienna, replicated then by the flight from the Nazis to the UK—could this be somehow preserved in the organisational DNA of a psychotherapy organisation like the Radcliffe? It was in the organisational genes? Or was he thinking this just to make himself feel better, to get over that sense of not being wanted? He wasn't sure. It was an interesting thought, for sure, but somehow thinking this over deprived him of the sense of pleasure in the progress made by his own patient, in his own psychodynamic work, and he considered this and frowned. He stood up, looking at himself in the mirror. The frown marks, he noted, were deepening ... and was that some grey in his black hair? He thought it was. The sense of time passing, with no real progress in his professional life, in improving his clinical capacity, upset him.

# TEN

It was June. The new job had become more routine. All seemed much as usual; Jack and Marie's baby arrived, just a few days late. David visited them with Rachel, on a hot sunny day. The new baby was a boy, christened for Jack's grandfather, Peter. Their front room was festooned with cards and flowers and the new parents were beaming but shocked by the sudden change to their lives. The tiny baby dozed fitfully with occasional dreams and whimpers. As David had feared, the sight of the happy new family provoked Rachel into a fresh assault on his determination not to go down the path of having a baby themselves.

"But why not, David?" Rachel said to him as they arrived back in their flat.

"I just feel I'm not ready to be a parent, Rachel," he said, nettled by the pressure from her.

"Well I can't carry on like this, hoping you'll change your mind," Rachel said, clearly hurt, yet again, and downcast. "What future do we have as a couple, if you won't really commit yourself to the future?"

David felt that she was right. It was crunch point. He didn't feel that he could see himself in the future, with children, with Rachel. It just didn't seem that they were sufficiently suited, and he had to admit to himself that he had drifted into the relationship with her, without consciously willing it. He was still aware that he was attracted to Clara … they had so much more in common, with their mutual interest in professional life. He tried to change the subject, to talk about their summer holiday, and then to talk about the possibility of decorating one of the rooms in their flat, but she wasn't to be easily distracted, again, he thought, with some justification.

"Do you think we have a future together, David?" she pressed him.

"That's a very big question, Rachel … just because Jack and Marie start a family, that doesn't mean that we have to … and I want to apply to the Radcliffe again …"

"The two aren't mutually exclusive, you know! Applying to the Radcliffe doesn't mean we can't start a family!"

"Well, look, I just don't feel ready. I'm sorry. In a way it's up to you what you want to do about that. You can wait, continue the relationship with me and just hope that I'll change my mind … or we could go our separate ways." He waited to see how she would react. He knew that he was being obdurate, just not going along with what she wanted. He didn't know if he was somehow waiting to see if the relationship between Clara and her psychotherapist partner Georg foundered …

"The trouble with you, David," said Rachel ominously and with some venom, "is that you don't want the commitment."

He could only agree. Later, as they strolled in the summer warmth of the park, he apologised for his lack of commitment and repeated that perhaps she felt that she could not continue the relationship with him. She did not respond directly, but it was clear that she did not want to leave him. He was grateful for that. He felt adrift, liking his job, his private practice, but not really having a way forward with his professional development since he had been turned down by the Radcliffe. He felt that his sense of drift was slightly vertiginous, and he carried on with his normal routine as in a dream, unable to orientate himself and with no sense of forward momentum. As June turned into July, and the familiar business overcame the child and adolescent service of referrals coming in thick and fast as the end of term approached, he was glad that the summer break was near. He found it debilitating, this sense of forward momentum in his career having been taken away from him with the Radcliffe's refusal to entertain the possibility of his training as a psychotherapist. He decided that in the autumn he would apply for seminars to become a senior member of his own counselling association, and having thought this he felt more enlivened and able to enjoy the summer holiday. He and Rachel had agreed to take a gite in France with Jack and Marie and their new baby Peter, and he enjoyed the routine of going out in the morning for leisurely trips and returning to the house in the hot afternoons for a rest, followed by another foray in the evening to a restaurant or for a stroll.

One morning they were walking across a dry hillside towards a line of trees and found, to their enchantment, a pool of clear water under the trees, fed by a spring sparkling down from the rocks above. The dry heat all around accentuated the smell of the pine trees standing on a rise of land by the flat sandy rocks that surrounded the little pool.

"This is just like *Jean de Florette*," said Jack, as he tenderly extracted baby Peter from the sling in which he had been carrying him. "Oh, now, are you hot?" he asked as the baby gave a little cry, scrunching up his features and looking likely to settle into a prolonged wail.

"Give him to me, Jack," said Marie, and got him settled at the breast, sitting on a rock in the shade at the edge of the pool, a bit like, David thought, the little mermaid of Copenhagen—but with a baby at the breast.

"*Jean de Florette*—that's a very tragic film about a man dying after the water's blocked from his farm, isn't it?" Rachel said.

"I saw it not so long ago. It could have been set here, these dry hills and now this lovely pool. And what a clear spring feeding down into it, just flooding out of the rock." She clambered up to where the water gushed out, splashing her face with it. All around the cicadas crisped, the sound seeming to rise in waves around them.

"*Spendidior vitro*," said David and Rachel splattered him with water, laughing.

"I sense a quotation coming on," she said. "Who is it this time? Horace?"

"Sweet water worthy of flowers," David continued unperturbed, wiping the water from his face. "Poet's writing about a spring, clearer than glass, and he says worthy of being garlanded with flowers. You can hear the onomatopoeia in the words. It sounds like water rippling."

"Well, that's a more cheerful thought than the man dying after his water was blocked," said Jack. "Who blocked the water, and why?"

"Oh, it was some competitors, who wanted the water to use for their own crops—they were growing carnations, I think," said Rachel.

"Maybe that's a bit like the Radcliffe. They don't want to allow too many people to train as psychotherapists so that there won't be too much competition," David said, letting rills of water run through his fingers from the cascade into the pool.

"In all seriousness, I think there may be something in that, you know," Marie said, looking up from her focus on the baby. She was on maternity leave and was missing her work, taken though she was with Peter, who sucked busily away at her breast as though he were a small workman tackling a very important task. "Oh, come on, David!" Jack said. "I don't think it's about stopping people training—I think it's more that they want to keep the Radcliffe small—at least, some people do—they want to make it exclusive".

"It's certainly that."

"Yes, I think that's right," said Marie, pushing strands of fair hair away from her face, which was dappled in the sunlight lancing through the leaves overhead. "But that's going to have to change … there aren't enough psychotherapists to train others already, certainly not in the Spaltung set, isn't that right Jack?"

"That is what I've heard," said Jack. He glanced at Rachel who was left out of this shop talk, and it was clear that a slight frigidity had descended on her as she gazed at the beautifully clear water of the pool. "But let's talk of something else," he added lightly. "What are we going to do for lunch? Shall we go back to the house and have some food?"

They strolled back to the house, chatting, with baby Peter settled in his sling and sleepy after his feed.

Back at work in September and into the usual routine after the holiday, David set up the therapy group for adolescents he and a child psychotherapy colleague had decided to run. He was bemused to discover that there had been redecorations over the summer, the corridor now a deep pink, which clashed with the rather bright turquoise of the group room they were going to use. In the first staff meeting of September, when all the team were together for the first time after the holidays, there was a good deal of dissatisfaction that they had not been consulted by the NHS department for "Facilities and Estates Management" over the colours to be used.

"I was consulted," said the principal child psychotherapist, Frieda, laughing. "I was actually in my room when they arrived with the paint. When I saw the paint for my room was lavender-coloured I refused to allow the workmen to use it. I insisted on cream."

"Were they using leftover paint—or what?" said the principal family therapist, an African-Caribbean woman of generally steady good humour, but now clearly upset. The group room doubled as a family therapy room with a one-way screen that could be covered with a plastic roll-down shutter when not in use, and she was not happy with the new pink colour.

"Well, look, it's good that we've been redecorated at all," said Thea, the child psychiatrist, diplomatically. "It's a bit of a shame that we weren't consulted, but I suspect that we'll soon get used to it."

And they did. It wasn't long before David hardly noticed that his room with its green rug on the floor and its blue chairs was not harmoniously colour-coded with the violent pink of the corridor walls. This was where he and Selena, his child psychotherapy colleague, met one day to talk over the group, to finalise dates and times, and to write to the young participants inviting them to come to the first meeting. Selena was a tall, dignified, rather stately woman who had told him that her mother was Spanish. She had trained at the Limes clinic and David had been impressed by her clinical flair and obvious intelligence. He thought that he could not be running the group with anyone more competent. He felt quite nervous—he had not run such a group before—and he felt that young people, with their mercurial states of mind, might be quite difficult to contain. Confiding something of his worry to Selena he was relieved that she, too, felt apprehensive, but she was convinced of the value of the group. She described the adolescent need to be identified with peers, and her sense that several of the group members, despite their difficulties, would fight shy of being involved in individual therapy sessions. They would feel less threatened in a group. David could not but agree, thinking of the difficulty he had often had in engaging young people in therapy even though he knew that it would be helpful for them.

The group was quite a mixed one. A white British girl, from a deprived East End family, Tina, of obvious intelligence and a likeable sense of fun, was their first choice for the group. Outgoing and lively, she might help to provide an atmosphere that would normalise ordinary discussion. Her background was a difficult one, and impulsively she had self-harmed a month previously after her mother left home to set up an alternative household with a new partner. She was fifteen. There was a black African boy, Ed, of a similar age, who was more worrying. He had thrown stones at people from some bins at the back of his block of flats in a fit of rage with his father, who had been angry with him over some failure to be sufficiently attentive to his academic work at school. He was a quiet lad, but David had the feeling he might be quite a handful once the group got under way. There was a Turkish girl, Sevda, who was also in difficulty with academic pressure at home. Her father was threatening to send her to family in Turkey if she did not attend more to her school work and make sure she came straight home from school rather than waywardly wandering off for a couple of hours with her school friends. There was a small, mousy-looking boy, Victor, from Poland, who despite his small size was fifteen, and who was being bullied at school. This having been sorted out and remedied, he was thought now to be quite depressed and David was certain this was right. Another girl, Vi, again white British, was rather wild and impetuous and given to being rude to the teachers in school and sobbing loudly whenever taken to task. It was felt that her social skills were rather lacking and an attempt was being made to assess her academic ability since it was felt that she was behind in her educational attainment.

"Well, we have quite a group, don't you think, Selena?" David said and they agreed that they would meet weekly with an open agenda, aiming to help the young people with their emotional difficulties. To this end they would focus on commenting on the process of the group as time went on, and would give the group a life of a year.

It was with a certain sense of anxiety that the group assembled for the first time. The young people were clearly nervous, despite the fact that they had already met both David and Selena. They looked sideways at each other, sizing each other up. Tina, as expected, led the way.

"Is your name Serene?" she demanded of Selena, despite the fact that David and she had just reintroduced themselves. Selena smiled and remarked,

"You might be wondering what sort of person I am. Am I very calm? Actually my name is Selena." Tina grinned and giggled. Gradually the group got started on the business of introducing themselves and beginning to get to know each other. It was noticeable that Ed, the black African boy, looked angry and didn't seem to want to be there. Victor looked very nervous indeed and tapped his foot without pause throughout the hour that they met. The girls were more talkative and made common cause in disparaging the colour of the walls, and in making personal comments about Selena's attire. David escaped this sort of attention.

After the group had finished David and Selena compared notes, talking together about the way the group had gone. There was also a useful chance to talk over the group in a clinical discussion with the rest of the team who had been responsible for referring into it. David found this discussion illuminating. Despite the huge pressure of work the team was under, and the pressure to dispense with this weekly clinical discussion slot in the team meeting, the consensus was that it was vital to support the clinicians in their work.

At about this time David was accepted for the course leading to senior membership of the psychodynamic counselling association he belonged to. The course would start in the spring term, and he needed to have two three-times-a week patients in treatment with him. He had Hugh, but he either needed a patient who wanted to come three times a week or he needed

to encourage one of his existing patients to come more often—
appropriately, where this was needed. He was pleased to be
moving ahead with his professional development and his
progress lessened the sting of the rejection by the Radcliffe. In
any case, he could keep applying, and he felt quietly confident
that he would be accepted at some point. Surely! His current
supervisor, a psychotherapist, was kind enough to say that she
felt that the Radcliffe would be acting against their best interests if they rejected him again, since he was so obviously competent and would have a lot to offer the organisation.

David commented to himself as he drove to work one Monday
morning that his professional development was not being
mirrored by progress in his relationship with Rachel. In her
early thirties, she was bored with her job in the bank, and was
increasingly dissatisfied with David's refusal to start a family,
even to move from their rather modest flat into a house. In desperation she suggested, over dinner one evening, that they
seek some marital therapy. David's heart sank. He knew that
the end of this process might very well be that they separated.
And who could blame Rachel in the face of his ambivalence?
Why should she waste her time on a partner whose gaze was
fixed elsewhere—his professional life, she thought, unaware
of the secret hold that Clara had on his affections. So it was
that they found themselves visiting a marital therapist who
worked privately, something David had insisted on as he felt
well known in the field.

The marital therapist's name was Francis Stewart. David liked
him on sight. He knew that he was a Radcliffe-trained consultant in a psychotherapy department as well as a marital
therapist, and this was a dual recommendation, David being
given to idealising the Radcliffe despite the problems he had
experienced. Francis was red-haired, angular, and kind. Rachel
gave a voluble account of her dissatisfactions with David.

David looked around. The room was clearly a study as well as a consulting room, a fine big room overlooking a small court-yard garden, sunlit, with large sofas and a coffee table. David felt comfortable, the more so when Francis said slightly quiz-zically that Rachel seemed for her part to feel that the issue was all David's fault. Rachel stopped, rather crestfallen, and Francis quickly went on to interpose a comment about couples often beginning their marital therapy with one of the couple carrying something of the responsibility for both. David said with a determination to move things on that he felt that Rachel had a point: she wanted to start a family and he didn't. Francis said that he wondered if that was because he wasn't com-mitted to the relationship, or didn't feel ready ... or? David was pleased to be able to elaborate his reasons in the safety of this setting, where he knew that Rachel would not become too vehement as she rehearsed yet again the reasons why they should start a family now and how cruel he was being to deny her. He knew his reasons sounded thin—not being ready, to his ears, sounded rather lame—but Francis listened carefully and he felt that he was not being blamed for his reluctance so much as given a space where all the complexities of his think-ing could be explored. It did seem odd, Francis said in a careful way, that they had come to this point in their relationship and now felt that they needed help to move on. Could it be that there might be some explanation for this block, might it relate to the history of their relationship? How had they met, what attracted them to each other first of all?

David described the choir, his awareness of the attractive soprano, and Rachel laughed, pleased to have this descrip-tion of her attractiveness brought into the open. Francis turned to Rachel. What about her? What had attracted her to David? Rachel laughed and impulsively said that they both had Presbyterian grandfathers. Francis looked surprised. David helped Rachel by clarifying that they both had quite a

Protestant work ethic, sometimes neither was home until eight in the evening. They did tend towards working twelve-hour days. Francis thought for a minute, looking out into the garden. Quietly he said that he thought that couples who tested their powers of endurance in this way might be avoiding something ... were they overworking in order to avoid arriving at a decision about ways to move forward in their relationship? Might this be a defensive manoeuvre on both their parts? Could it be that Rachel, on meeting David, had noticed that he was on the same wavelength as her in relation to using work as a way of dealing with personal matters? David agreed with him but Rachel was inclined to go back to her complaint about David being the one who threw a spanner in the works ... and the session continued in the same vein. As they left, Rachel and David both agreed that they felt that it had been helpful. It had opened up a space for them to think through the issues between them in a way that wasn't too fraught. David was surprised and pleased. He felt that he might be able to offer the thoughts he had about not feeling able to commit himself without it being too devastating for Rachel. He felt it might be possible for them to arrive at some sort of agreement, maybe to defer the decision for a while, for her to lessen the pressure on him. He felt concerned to maintain what was good about their relationship—not, he joked to himself, to throw the baby out with the bathwater. He was optimistic.

In fact he was wrong. Some weeks into the discussions he talked about not wanting to have children with Rachel. She was deeply troubled—and moved out. Clearly the process of the discussions had been sufficient for her to get in touch with the bitter disappointment she felt in David's attitude to their joint life together, and without any fuss she quietly took some of her things and moved to her parent's house in the Chilterns. She rang David and explained that she did not feel able to continue and would rather they separated. She arranged a time with him to pick up her things. David felt relieved, to his surprise. He felt liberated, but sad that he had not been able to join in with her thoughts about their future together. He went to work on the Monday morning with the sense of relief giving him a lightness in mood. He found his thoughts turning to Clara, and he lamented all over again the fact that he had not acted quickly enough to secure her against the involvement of Georg. Politely, he went to a session with Francis without Rachel. Francis was sympathetic, but David could tell he was unsurprised, both at the news that Rachel had left him, and at the fact that she chose not to come to the session. Francis did not comment on what Rachel had said to him although he did say that she had telephoned to let him know that she would not be coming to any further sessions.

# ELEVEN

It wasn't long after he and Rachel had split up that he found himself at a meeting at the Limes clinic about a new research project that was being proposed. He noticed that Clara was sitting in the front row and at a suitable moment he found his way towards her. She was obviously pleased to see him. David told her that he had moved on from his relationship with Rachel, whom Clara had encountered a few times at social events to which they had all been invited.

"I hope it's not too difficult for you, David," she said with a warmth and sincerity that surprised him, looking at him with her clear green eyes, which he felt were quite unique. Nobody else could have eyes of that colour. He realised that he was staring at her wordlessly while he entertained the thought about her eyes, and, embarrassed, he was stilted and awkward in his response.

"It *is* a major a change. Difficult too being turned down again by the Radcliffe."

"What, again?" she said indignantly. "Why don't they know what's good for them?"

He felt uncomfortable about her vehemence on this subject and he thought that there was probably a story there about her own relationship with the Radcliffe.

"How's your training going? Nearly finished yet?" he asked.

"I'm getting there. It's very exhausting though. Not much time for anything else. I'm going to move over into private practice as soon as I can, away from the NHS."

"I can't say I blame you. It's a struggle in the public sector with all the cuts coming on stream and the waiting lists growing all the time … constant pressure."

"Yes … and with Georg having decided to teach more in Switzerland I shall have more time to myself." She looked sideways at him. He wondered for a moment if he was being given a hint that their relationship was in trouble. Frustratingly, he couldn't tell; she was opacity itself, and instantly turned the conversation to something else. He told himself that it was too much to hope for, that she might be free to have a relationship with him when he himself was free. They were interrupted by the meeting continuing. Afterwards, he joined up with her again and they talked about the research project and neutral matters as they walked down the stairs together. Then someone else cut in on their conversation and he found himself on the street outside, unsettled, and wondering how he might engineer another meeting with her … then he told himself roughly that he was being quite unrealistic, that he couldn't hope to link up with her—and went home to his flat.

The flat was full of Rachel's presence: her belongings had gone now, but he could see the parts of the flat they had decorated together, the rug they had chosen together, and even the duvet cover on the bed was one they had chosen together. He sighed and set about the business of cooking supper and preparing for work next day. He was glad when the phone rang and Jack's voice broke in upon his mood, which he had felt was beginning to be a depressed one. Jack sounded very tired, and it was clear that parenthood and the training, as well as the work at the Limes clinic, was taking all his energy. David had noticed that they were meeting less frequently than before. Charitably, he hoped that it was the new-parent experience, but at less charitable moments he felt that he was being side-lined in favour of Jack's training and professional life. They still ran together, though, and David valued his role as honorary uncle to their child. Jack asked him if he was going to apply again and David hesitated.

"I think so," he said. "I'm not quite sure whether to leave it until I've done the post-qualifying course."

"Yes ... I think the timing of these things is difficult. But there's a change of membership in the group of people that deals with applications ... that might help you, might be a favourable wind, so to speak."

"True. D'you know who's in the group now?" David was relieved at the names given him by Jack. He knew them and he thought they were a lively group, more interested, he hoped, in widening their scope in considering applicants. "I do feel inclined just to press on with another application," he said. "I can't believe they'd turn me down a third time, there doesn't seem any particular reason for it."

"Did they give you any clues as to why you were turned down the last time?" Jack asked, and David reminded him that he had been told that he wasn't sufficiently interested in becoming a psychotherapist. He had said guilelessly that he would in all likelihood continue in the NHS half-time if he were to train as a psychotherapist, only latterly realising that this would be seen as evidence of a lack of commitment. Jack had also told him afterwards that this would be regarded negatively by the real acolytes of the Radcliffe; it would have been politic to have indicated a total commitment to the life of a psychotherapist despite the financial sacrifices that this would entail. Few psychotherapists made a lucrative business of private practice, and he knew many who were supported by spouses who worked steadily at a "proper job". Or had private means. David had thought that he would continue half-time in the NHS, since this would provide some financial back up. He told himself, ironically, that had he continued in the relationship with Rachel he would have had no financial strain to worry about because of her work in the bank.

"Well, I'll think about putting in another application," David said, and asked Jack if he would be interested in sailing the next weekend. David and Rachel had begun to join Jack and Marie at the cottage Jack's family owned on the south coast, for weekends sailing and walking. Even with the baby, Jack seemed to want to continue in this tradition. They arranged to travel down together on the Friday night and it was a pleasure for David to see that the weather-forecast was favourable.

As they put the dinghy in the water at Bosham, the little jetty was busy with other sailors getting their boats ready, the slap of rigging against mast gentle but insistent in the pleasant autumn breeze. They set out for a brief sail around Chichester harbour, David crewing, and Jack being very efficient at the tiller, with the need to avoid moored yachts and other boats. Later on, as they were coming back to Bosham with the flood tide, the wind freshened, and the boat began to be more lively, water chuckling under the bows with a higher note. David was looking forward past the sail to the rise of the South Downs, the thought of lunch beginning to be appealing. He wondered if Marie would have had time to sort out something good to eat as well as looking after baby Peter.

"Better both sit out," said Jack suddenly. "Looks like a bit of a squall coming." Sure enough, David could see a darker line ruffling the water where the wind was getting up. He levered himself up on to the thwart, tucking his feet under the toe-strap to hold his balance, feeling Jack sitting up beside him and tucking his toes under the strap too. David jerked the jib-sheet out of its cleat so that he could let it fly free if they heeled over too much.

"Here it comes," said Jack, and David was aware of the boat tipping suddenly as the squall hit them. He leant out hard, arching his back and hanging on with his feet under the toe-strap. Suddenly there was a snapping noise as the fixing of the toe-strap broke. The boat sheered away from them as both he and Jack, inelegantly and side-by-side, somersaulted backwards into the water. The boat stayed upright for a second then tipped over just ahead of them. Fortunately, Jack still had hold of one of the sheets. The water was shockingly cold.

"Oh God!" said Jack, spluttering and beginning to swim to the boat. "I knew I should've replaced the screws for the strap … they were getting a bit worn."

"Yes, you should've," muttered David under his breath, aware that the occupants of a nearby boat were calling to offer assistance while at the same time laughing at their plight.

Mortifying, he thought to himself as they laboriously righted the boat and bailed her out a little. Jack got the boat moving again before the wind, which was once more reasonably light, and the water in her streamed out of the panels at the stern. David bailed furiously.

"Call it a day, I think," said Jack, laughing. "We need to get in and have a hot shower."

They squelched on to the slipway and pulled the boat out of the water.

"Don't often see that," said the harbourmaster, a grizzled elderly man who was smiling sympathetically. "Are you alright?"

"We're fine," said Jack. "Toe-strap fixing went. Just very wet."

"Happens to the best of us. Luckily you were quite near base," said the harbourmaster, helping them with the last yard or two of pulling the boat in. "You can shower in the clubhouse if you want."

"Well that's kind, but we aren't far from home. We'll leave the boat here and get home to shower and have lunch," Jack said, his teeth beginning to chatter slightly in the breeze.

Over lunch, David joked,

"Not every day you lose a girlfriend and get a dunking in the sea," he said. He felt gloomy. After the weekend it would be back to work. He was very much aware that Jack and Marie were happy together, with Peter a much-adored baby whose chuckles and gurgles filled both parents with first-time-parenthood pride. He was glad to get back to his flat the next evening. He turned his thoughts to the working week. First, it was the adolescent group, and he groaned to himself. He was finding them alarming, and however much he might tell himself that his reaction was part of what they felt, lodged in *him*, their anxiety about being in this unfamiliar group therapy setting being got rid of by dint of making *him* feel anxious, he felt that, actually, his inexperience in running groups, especially for this age group, was a difficulty.

But he was pleased to be working with Selena; he felt she was confident and well-trained; he envied her the child psychotherapy training she'd had at the Limes clinic. He had found the baby observation seminars he had taken part in there had been impressive and that his clinical capacity had deepened as a result. And the group *had* settled somewhat. One of its members, Ed, had dropped out and actually David was relieved, as he had seemed to become increasingly withdrawn and had looked angry much of the time. David and Selena felt the aggressive stance was sufficiently worrying to alert Thea, the child psychiatrist, who, after some weeks, offered a review to Ed and his parents. They were concerned about their son, and made sure he attended the appointment. He said he didn't want to return to the group but did agree to further regular appointments with his family to see the psychiatrist. So that was the most troubled member of the group taken care of, said David to himself.

In this meeting, the members of the group seemed in high spirits and joked a lot. In fact, there was a lot of dancing around and Vi, whose sober dress belied her tendency towards getting over-excited, did an impromptu song and dance routine.

"Aren't the rest of you going to dance?" she laughed, throwing her arms around. The Polish boy, Victor, looked positively alarmed and shrank into his seat. The others also pretended not to hear her, and one of them caught Vi as she overreached herself and tipped sideways on to the floor.

"Perhaps you're wondering if we can manage such high spirits," said David, thinking to himself as he made this remark that this was certainly something *he* was wondering about, and it was a feeling that was coming from him, and was based on his inexperience rather than being lodged in him from the atmosphere in the group. Tina looked at him thoughtfully. She was easily the most reflective member of the group, as well as the most mature.

"Well it's true that if we were at school now Vi would be in a lot of trouble. Don't you think, Vi?" she turned to Vi and nudged her with her elbow. Vi giggled. Victor sighed audibly and looked out of the window. He felt in his pocket and brought out a little computer toy and started to distance himself from what was going on, clearly entranced with it.

"I know what that is, Victor," said Sevda, the Turkish girl. "It's one of those things you have a programme on, it's a little game. Isn't that right?" Victor nodded. She went on. "Well, one, I don't think you should be playing with it instead of joining in with the conversation, and two, we're not allowed those in school so you shouldn't have it here."

David noted to himself that Victor seemed to have tapped into rather an authoritarian streak in Sevda. Vi grabbed the toy from Victor.

"Oh my God," she said dramatically, looking alarmed as she studied it.

"Please can I have it back?" said Victor. She gave it back to him, playfully tossing it to him.

"You realise that game is like to finish?" she said playfully. "It needs activity!"

"Well, he can't play the game if you throw it round like that," said Sevda.

"There do seem to be ideas in the group about how a game should be kept going, looked after," said Selena, filling David with admiration at how quickly she had picked up on the meaning of the exchange. "Perhaps it says something about how each of you feels about whether you are going to get looked after in this group, going to get helped or not, with the difficulties each of you brings." Victor looked blank and immersed himself in pressing the buttons on the toy. Vi looked as though she didn't understand what Selena was saying. Tina looked thoughtful again and David decided that she represented the thinking function of the group, that she alone of them seemed to be prepared to give consideration to what he and Selena said, whereas the others seemed disinterested or determined to block out what was being communicated.

"Well, we're not talking about how we come to be here, are we?" Tina looked at Victor who said nothing, twitching his foot nervously. "I don't know why you others are here at all. I'm quite curious. Don't you others want to know about me, why I'm here?"

David held his breath. It might be that the group, some weeks in, could begin to talk honestly together about themselves. There was an anxious silence. The others clearly couldn't countenance the idea of talking openly in a situation that was so alarming. David broke the silence.

"There might be differences between you about how much each of you wants to say about what brings you to the group," he said. "Tina feels that it would be useful, move things on, to talk together openly about why you're here. You others don't share that opinion, by the look of it. Might be a bit frightening to talk openly with each other."

The mood of the group had changed very significantly from the over-excited and jokey state that had prevailed in the beginning. The young people were quite serious now, and each of them seemed to be thinking. David felt pleased that they seemed to be in the realm of thought rather than in the realm of action. He found it alarming when there was dancing around and things threatened to get out of control. There was more silence. Tina broke it by saying something bright about the colour of Selena's shirt—where had she got it? David sighed inwardly at this blatant change of subject and reflected that, perhaps for this session at least, a little thinking work had been done, a view he found Serena shared when they discussed the group afterwards.

# TWELVE

Not long after this David decided to put in another application to the Radcliffe. His first interview was with an elderly man, a tall stooped figure with wisps of grey hair creating a halo effect around his head. His consulting room in a leafy street was extremely dark, and slightly dank, even allowing for the fact that it was November and the weather was gloomy. David had the impression that he was entering a cellar. It was a dark room anyway, overshadowed by lime trees growing close to the house, and the two dim table lamps on polished antique side tables did little to lessen the dimness. The interview started in a way that took David aback. Andrew Coulterden had a sheaf of papers in his hand, which he waved at David as they sat down.

"I've read your application form and the reports of your previous interviews," he said. "Quite frankly, I have to tell you that some psychotherapists would regard you as hardly treatable, let alone suitable to train as a therapist."

David's jaw tightened. "What makes you say that?" he asked, as coolly as he could.

"It's your history of disturbance—trying to crash your car— you weren't even an adolescent, which would go some way to explaining such instability," he said. "I think you only have a fifty per cent chance of this application being successful."

David assumed that this meant that his mind was made up, as he had two interviews and presumably this was the first fifty per cent.

"Surely, if I've been interviewed a number of times—and found a training therapist—there must be some sense in the organisation that I am suitable," he protested, with an edge to his voice that he could not disguise.

"It's so useful for applicants to be looked at by different people from the Radcliffe," said Coulterden easily, smilingly brushing away David's comment. David felt tempted to remark on the incoherence of the process.

"I have had two psychotherapists so far," he said, "and neither of them seem to have had any reservations about offering me treatment, nor about my applying to the Radcliffe."

Coulterden's warm and pleasant manner did not shift. He shuffled in his chair, stretching his legs out comfortably.

"Oh, of course, people have different views. I'm not saying they don't. But they're hardly going to comment if there's something wrong under the bonnet ... like a good mechanic, who doesn't explain the detail of what's wrong with the car, just gives a general impression."

"But I'm not a car!" David had a distressing sense that he was being pushed into being someone whose reaction to this kind of provocative statement could be seen and labelled as pathological. There was a short silence.

"Of course, you could train with another organisation, probably, just not the Radcliffe," said Coulterden.

"I have already trained as a psychodynamic counsellor. In fact I've been working as one for some time," said David. "And I've been doing a post-qualifying course to enhance my practice."

"I am sure that's very beneficial for you," Coulterden said soothingly. "I don't mean to imply that you aren't a competent professional in your field. All I'm saying is that some therapists would feel that you're not treatable with your history. Or that

you might be treatable ... but it would take a very long time."
David's exasperation got the better of him and he laughed at
what he thought was a ridiculous way of dismissing his application. Coulterden held up a warning hand.

"Look, I think that what I'm saying is a shock to you. Perhaps
no one has said to you before that you are clearly someone
with a disturbance, a disturbance severe enough to make some
therapists feel that you might not be treatable, and certainly
not suitable to train at the Radcliffe."

"You're right about that," David said with some heat. "If
you feel that I'm hardly treatable, that doesn't seem to be
a view shared by my two therapists, and indeed by some of
the therapists who interviewed me for the course. And I was
found a training psychotherapist."

"But they did turn you down," Coulterden said quickly.
"Their reports agree broadly with my view." There was nothing
to be said to that. There was a pause. "At any rate," Coulterden
added as though this would be the clincher, "the Radcliffe is
only accepting academics to train now. Your academic qualifications aren't sufficient."

"If that's the case," David said, "why was I allowed to put in
a new application? I stated clearly what my qualifications were:
first degree, postgraduate degree in clinical psychology, training in psychodynamic counselling, and many years of practice
supervised by psychotherapists." David's mood was becoming
as dark as the lighting in the room. He began to have the sensa-
tion that he was struggling in a quicksand. "It does sound as
though your mind was made up even before you started interviewing me," he said quickly, trying to remain calm and upbeat.
"Have you read the references from the therapists who wrote
them for me?" he asked, knowing that he was wasting his time.

"Yes—and in fact they wrote you good references."
Coulterden's tone indicated that he was surprised by this.
"Look, I don't think we should prolong this interview. You've

got another interview to come, haven't you, and then we'll have a discussion in the group about your application. Mind you, groups being what they are, the discussion isn't likely to be helpful to you. Shall we leave it there?" David saw no point in continuing the conversation. He allowed himself to be shown the door, and found himself on the pavement, furious.

He wondered why he was bothering to struggle to be accepted by an organisation whose representatives behaved like this. Why had he been allowed to apply if the goalposts had now changed and he needed further academic qualifications? And what sort of qualifications? His masters in clinical psychology clearly did not count … perhaps only doctorates, like Clara with her psychology doctorate? On impulse he picked up his mobile phone and called her. She was working but said she would call him back that evening.

That evening he sat in the window of his flat, looking out into the garden at the dismal drizzle falling on the broken, blackened stumps of last year's plants, and waited for Clara to call. When she did, she invited him round and as he went he realised that under any other circumstance he would have been delighted. He had not often been to her house on his own; only to dinners and to a party to celebrate Georg's fiftieth birthday—this an odd occasion, as he would not have said he knew Georg except as a dinner party companion. Clara was at the door to greet him, her cat alertly at her side. The tiled floor of the hall resounded harshly under his shoes as she showed him into the grand living room, a double room with fireplaces adorned with patterned Edwardian tiles. A fire was burning brightly in one of the fireplaces, and the cat stretched out in front of it as they sat down, spreading its paws out blissfully towards the warmth of the blaze.

"No Georg?" he asked, as they sat down.

"No, he's in Switzerland at the moment, doing some teaching," Clara said composedly. "Would you like a drink? A coffee, or a glass of wine?"

"I wouldn't mind a glass of wine," David said, and waited while she went into the kitchen, coming back with a glass in each hand.

"I thought I'd join you with the wine," she said. "You don't look good. Do you want to tell me what happened with Andrew Coulterden?"

"It was kind of you to invite me round. I do feel wretched about it. D'you know what he said? He said they were only accepting academics now."

"That's such nonsense!" Clara said, laughing. "That simply isn't true." She paused, as though wondering whether to tell him something. "You know, don't you, about Andrew Coulterden's reputation?"

"No ... I know he's very elderly—he seems a nice enough person."

"The difficulty is that he's very traditional in his views, hasn't been brought into the modern world ... I had him for some seminars, and he said that I seemed quite intelligent for someone who came from the Spaltung group."

"Maybe he's a bit of a maverick, then," replied David. He sipped his wine, feeling it beginning to warm the chilly sense of misery and anger that had engulfed him.

"Oh, I wouldn't take it personally that he's behaved like this. He might be chair of the group that deals with new applications, but he's well known as someone who's—well, a bit old-fashioned."

"For God's sake!" David sprang to his feet in exasperation. The cat, startled, rose to its feet, prepared to flee. "Oh, it's alright," he said, bending down to stroke it. "What's he worried for? I'm not the sort to kick the cat."

"She," Clara corrected him. "She's a nervy little thing."

"Oh. Not like her owner, a calm, steady person, eh?"

"Oh, of course," she said, laughing. "But look, just because Andrew Coulterden treats you like this, it's not a done deal. Who's your next interview with?"

"Lewis Wray," David said, looking at her anxiously. What did Clara know about him? "Do you know anything about him, his reputation?"

"Well, you haven't struck it particularly lucky with him either," said Clara, looking worried. "He does have a reputation for wanting to keep the Radcliffe small, just as it is. There's actually beginning to be a body of opinion about the way that people who are perfectly suitable keep getting turned down, but it's a small group ... most people feel that there's going to have to be something quite special about you to be accepted. Ordinary people—not wanted."

The conversation went on along the same lines; Clara was sympathetic and listened intently as he gave her a picture of the way the interview had gone. The one suggestion she made was something that he thought he might give serious consideration to: the idea of restarting psychotherapy. He thought that a therapy with a member of the Spaltung group would be very worthwhile. The attention to the here-and-now momentary shifts in the detail of the sessions would be worth developing more in his own work. It would be a sort of apprenticeship, as well as helpful in relation to the turbulence in his own state of mind, with his work, which was always stressful, and, of course, with his relationships. He could not get it out of his head that he wanted a relationship with Clara. It was heaven to be sitting with her in her living room, fire burning brightly, the conversation flowing easily between them, and her dark hair seeming almost to have a life of its own as it shone in the firelight.

He felt so much better after their conversation that he almost began to sing to himself on the way home. He was always amused by the fact that the choice of song he crooned quietly to himself—or more loudly in secluded settings like the kitchen when he was cooking—seemed to be entirely relevant to the state of his internal world at that moment. Tonight it was the trio from *Così fan tutte*; the farewell to the lovers setting sail on an ocean, which, it was to be hoped, would be tranquil. He smiled wryly to himself: he was departing from Clara, whom he wished was his lover. And if his previous contact with the Radcliffe was anything to go by, the journey wouldn't be tranquil in relation to his next interview. Certainly not if he were to be turned down. In fact (he embroidered the theme), he would be departing in earnest from the Radcliffe. He wouldn't apply again. A bit like being excommunicated from the church, if he were to be rejected again. But he enjoyed the music. The lovers in *Così* were pretending to depart, of course, but the farewell sung to them was no less heartfelt and poignant for that.

He had a fortnight to get through before his next interview. As usual, work was a solace, although the group for the adolescents was proving just as difficult as he had feared. This time Vi was proving even more difficult to contain than usual. She habitually danced about a lot and was voluble and excitable in each group, and all their comments about her wanting to avoid the more serious or ordinary concerns of the group, and what brought them there, seemed ineffectual. The only relief was that her behaviour at school had improved, so that it was clear, at least, that the group was providing a setting where her disturbance could be held. The others in the group were tolerant, although it was clear that Tina preferred to be speaking about matters of importance to her and to others rather than engaging in the energetic running about and dancing that Vi favoured. The Polish boy had taken to bringing paper and felt tips into the sessions and drawing intricate pictures that had begun to make sense in terms of the life of the group. It wasn't long before the Christmas break, and in the previous week's session the members of the group had been given the holiday break times, so that Selena and David were expecting some reaction now. It had become clear that the members of the group had begun to value it and to enjoy coming. They would miss it over the break.

As the group started, Victor, the Polish boy, sat down at one of the tables on the edge of the group as usual, getting out his felt tips and settling down to a very colourful drawing.

"It's Christmas drawing," he said. "It always snows in Poland." He had settled into the group, feeling able to talk, although nervous of Vi who was so lively, and of Sevda, the Turkish girl who tended to give him instructions. Being the only boy in the group was difficult for him, coming as he did from a family of brothers, but he persevered and seemed to like to sit near David if he could, studying him carefully. On one occasion he had done a portrait of David, catching the likeness rather well, with the black hair that was prone to flop over his forehead, the hazel eyes, and the slightly sharp nose.

On this occasion his snow scene developed into a rather sombre one, some trees with bare branches stabbing the sky, which was a dark blue sprinkled with yellow stars. Actually today the weather was foggy, the trees outside the window dripping clear drops on to the wet grass below, those further away receding into the dimness. Gradually, as the group progressed, David could see the pale disc of the sun beginning to emerge from the mist with a hint of blue in the sky. Not that he had much time to notice. When Selena commented on the bleakness in the picture, and the fact that the group might be feeling a little sad today, which did seem to be the prevailing atmosphere, Vi jumped to her feet. Unusually for her she had been sitting down, studying Selena's dress with frank curiosity and asking her where she had bought it. When this comment was made, however, she leapt to her feet and without apparent concern at the fact that she had tripped over Sevda's feet, ran to the low sink in the room and filled a plastic cup with water. She slopped and spilled it over the floor. Fortunately the floor was NHS-issue

125

vinyl—blue with little spangles of glittery stuff in it—and David found time to think to himself that it mirrored the silver in Victor's picture of the stars sparkling across the sky, just as Vi advanced towards him.

"Would you like to get wet?" she giggled, threatening him with the cup of water. "I think you need a bit of cooling down!"

"Oh, Vi!" said Tina with some exasperation. "Calm down! It wouldn't be nice for him to be spending the rest of the day soaking wet."

David froze, his thinking capacity momentarily overwhelmed, except that he could imagine only too well how it would be to spend the rest of the day in soaking clothes, with each patient or family in turn commenting. Fortunately Selena was quick-witted. At this moment she represented, of the two of them, the thinking part of the therapeutic couple they had become in relation to the group members.

"Well Vi, I think you must feel very upset by the fact that we are going to be stopping the group for the break," Selena said quickly. "I expect you all have some feelings about it. Perhaps you feel that you've had some cold water thrown over you. You're not happy about the break, are you? What are you going to be doing in the time? Do you have plans?"

Vi's impulsivity, and her difficulty in concentrating, was distinctly to David's advantage here, as she forgot that she had been threatening him, retreated to the sink, and poured the water away. With her back to them, she said that she was going to be staying with her mother ... it was going to be very boring. Extremely boring, in fact.

"So you're feeling the break is going to be quite difficult ... perhaps you others feel a bit the same," David said, recovering his capacity for thought now that the immediate threat of a soaking had been withdrawn. Vi looked unusually thoughtful, and, sitting down, began picking at the hem of her cardigan. "It's hard to bear with it, this feeling we won't be meeting for two weeks," David said. She nodded moodily.

126

"Well, I will be seeing some of my uncles and aunts," she said, her mood lifting a little. "They're coming over. We're going to cook a big meal. I like cooking, helping my Mum."

"Sounds like a nice thing to be doing," said Selena. Vi nodded, looking pleased. Victor looked at David shyly and David felt that he was being given a hint that the drawing was now ready for display and comment.

"Would you like to show us your drawing, Victor? Tell us about it?" David said. Actually Victor was quite a talented artist, and seemed to be beginning to discover that he could address his depression by producing drawings and paintings that brought him recognition and praise. If they had an art therapist on the team, thought David to himself, Victor would have found the sessions useful ... as it was, he contributed to the group with his drawings, which always seemed to have something of relevance to the general atmosphere to speak about. Victor seemed to find a quiet satisfaction in having his state of mind picked up on and talked about. A nourishing experience in fact, and this thought, as it crystallised in David's mind, gave him a way into talking about Victor's picture.

Victor picked up his picture by the edges and they could see that the blue sky and the black stabbing trees standing in the snow were shielding a house. Inside the house was a table, which seemed to be laden with delicious-looking food: a chicken on a plate, a pile of biscuits, steaming pots.

"This is a picture about Christmas time at my house," he said.

"Looks like there are lots of good things to eat," said David. "Maybe it's a picture of two halves, like a football game can be." Victor grinned, liking the reference to football, which could, as he had told David the previous week, be a game of two halves, each half very different. "The two halves here," David carried on, "could perhaps be about how you feel about the group. The bare trees, the cold snow, you and maybe the others are going to feel a bit out in the cold when you don't have the group to come to during the break. But inside the house, it's all cosy, lots of good food to eat." Victor nodded.

"Like what we eat at home at Christmas," he said.

"Exactly," said David. "And perhaps here in the group you all have a feeling that you can have a bit of a cosy time, nice things, and it's difficult to lose that over the break." Victor looked thoughtful. Sevda snorted and wandered over the window.

"Fog's clearing," she said. "Not so grey. But I think you people talk a load of rubbish. I'll be glad not to have to come here over the break. I'm not bothered. Am I bothered? No." She sat down again, glaring contemptuously, and Selena commented,

"You feel it's getting a bit brighter, perhaps you feel we can understand how you might feel sometimes ... but you also feel we get it wrong now and again."

"You certainly do," said Sevda with quiet satisfaction. "Most of the time in fact. You people need to get your act together." David sighed inwardly. He could imagine that Sevda might get told a lot of the time to get her act together, to work harder in school, to behave better. He knew from contact with the school that her behaviour and work were not improving, and that her father had been called in to the school to discuss their concerns.

"We need to improve, clearly, Sevda," he said. "And you feel we don't get it right here. Despite that, you come here every week, and you feel that we can bear with what you feel about us, the fact that you feel we're not getting it right." She grunted and stared out of the window.

It was time to stop, and as the young people trooped out, David felt some relief that he had survived the group without being soaked. It was also a relief to talk through the session with Selena.

# THIRTEEN

I t was when David was thinking of his next interview that he realised—or thought he did—the full implications of not being accepted this time. He had decided that it would be the end of his contact with the Radcliffe. He could carry on in the two settings he worked in. He could struggle to get a relationship going with Clara—but it would be undermined by the fact that she was a psychotherapist at a prestigious organisation while he wasn't. Similarly with Jack. Jack and Clara were in; he would be out. He supposed he could apply to a less prestigious organisation, but the Radcliffe was unique and in a leading position. There were other trainings across the world, several in cities in the States. He toyed momentarily with the idea of moving; perhaps he could pursue a career as a therapist there. But this was a big step to take … it would mean leaving everything behind—his relationships with friends, his family, his network of work colleagues built up over the years. And of course it would mean leaving Clara. He shrugged off this thought and, as it was the weekend, hurriedly organised himself to go for a run. It was spring again; the cold of the winter months, the dark days, were being left behind and it was bright but blowy, with clouds scudding across the sky. As he ran, David thought that the pigeons he could see being tossed and thrown about by the wind perhaps enjoyed it, and he felt his state of mind improving. His interview was the next day and he slept well, eager to get it over with and determined to make a good impression.

To David's surprise, Lewis Wray was young; he had become accustomed to being met by elderly therapists. He could not be more than forty, he surmised; fifty at most. He was a tall man, with mousy hair and a sharp face. He did not smile on meeting David, who said to himself that he was used to that. But at least he did speak to him, asking him about why he wished to train as a therapist. Gradually the familiar sense of unease began to set in as David realised that Wray was tending to contradict most of what he was saying. When asked if he liked to read Freud he replied that he had found reading Freud valuable in his training but was currently reading a book by one of the Spaltung set. If he were to be accepted he would look forward to discussing some of the ideas in seminars.

"If you are accepted, that is," Wray said acidly. He didn't quite know what to say to this. He looked around the room. It was clearly Wray's living room. The sun was shining in so brightly that he had needed to draw some of the curtains; squashy black sofas and polished wooden floorboards were brightly lit, as though by stage lighting. David felt Wray was somehow uncomfortable in this setting, and thought that it would have been more professional to have interviewed him in his consulting room. David felt he was being given a strong message that his application was not acceptable for some reason that he could not understand. Worse followed. Wray went on to say that, of course, David's social life would be ruined if he were not accepted. Again, he did not know what to say to this, other than to make a general statement that he did socialise with some therapists, but not exclusively. Then he was invited to describe his family life. To his consternation, Wray made mileage of the fact that David said he felt that his two younger sisters somehow belonged more in the family than he did, had closer relationships both with each other and

130

with their parents. Wray commented again rather coolly and unsympathetically, even, David thought, with schadenfreude, that if David were not to be accepted he would have to face that dynamic all over again, since others were being brought into the family, accepted into the Radcliffe, whilst he was not.

Wray went on to ask him if he planned to give up his public sector work if he were to be accepted and he said he would probably work half-time in the NHS and half-time as a therapist. This time he added that it would be financially necessary if he were to manage his mortgage, as the income from psychotherapeutic practice was uncertain, and not a generous one. This seemed to him self-evident. Wray clearly did not like this reply and just looked at him without speaking.

David's heart sank. He felt sure that he would not be accepted, and this impression was heightened when Wray remarked that at least David had his professional life. He began to wonder why they had bothered to interview him at all, since their minds were so obviously made up, and they so clearly felt that he was not acceptable. The thought struck him—an uncharitable one—that perhaps it swelled their coffers if they offered to interview anyone who applied who would pay the considerable fee. And the interpretative comments? Wild and intrusive, he thought. It wasn't appropriate to talk as these interviewers tended to, unless as part of an established therapy.

It wasn't a surprise when he received a letter some three months later saying that his application had not been successful. David was just very angry. He made an appointment to meet again with one of his interviewers, and chose Andrew Coulterden, on the basis that he was more likely to give away, chattily and in an unboundaried way, the reasons for his rejection. David himself could not see what the objection to his application was. He felt that he was as competent professionally as Jack and Clara; he had shown himself to be committed to psychodynamic thinking by training as a psychodynamic counsellor, and he had spent years—and many thousands of pounds—in psychotherapy. He also felt he brought with him a depth of understanding from having had to grapple with his own difficulties.

He challenged Andrew Coulterden straightaway. How could he have been interviewed again, if his academic qualifications were now regarded as insufficient? Coulterden changed the subject immediately, suggesting to David that he might be very disappointed to be turned down. David was used now to the way in which therapists failed to address the subject of a question and instead always answered with a comment about his state of mind.

"I am disappointed, and actually very surprised," he said. "I have good references from psychotherapists I have worked with, and I've had a lot of therapy as well as a lot of training."

"I'm sure your therapy has helped you," Coulterden said smoothly. "And good references … that's true, you do have good references, which is somewhat surprising really."

"Why is it surprising?" David asked. It was a waste of time, as he knew it would be. Transparency was not a quality that he had encountered in his attempts to be accepted by the Radcliffe.

"I just wonder how useful a meeting this is going to be," Coulterden said. "You know, you were thought by the committee not to be really interested in working as a therapist."

"On what basis?" David kept his voice even, although he was really very angry. On what basis could they possibly feel that he was not interested in working as a therapist? He worked very hard maintaining a private practice as well as working in the NHS … he imagined it must be because he had not said that he would work full time as a therapist. This must have been the slip that he again made. Did they not realise that it would be very difficult to earn a living as a therapist without a spouse to support his private practice and provide stability of income? Of course, Coulterden did not answer this question either, but it was immaterial, as David had already understood what the problem was.

"I can see that all the years of therapy I have had and paid for, and the work as a psychodynamic counsellor, don't count for much," David said, allowing some bitterness to show.

"I think it's very important to say that all your interviewers felt the same about you. We all felt that it was not appropriate to allow you to train as a therapist," Coulterden said.

"I wonder if it is possible to tell me why not?"

"You are right to use that word possible ..." Coulterden smiled at his own felicity of phrase. "Actually, it's not possible to say. It could be that we have made a mistake in your case ... we do make mistakes."

"If that is so, then what's going to be done about it?" asked David, feeling even as he said this that there was no point in pursuing the matter with this slippery character.

"Oh, well, if we have made a mistake we'll write to you."


Of course, there was no letter. David felt completely blocked. The frustration of it made him feel as if he was dragging a heavy weight around with him. It was helpful that Jack commented that the Radcliffe was, itself, a body excluded from the life of the society in which it had its being, and its routine rejection of candidates whom most people felt were suitable for training performed a function for the organisation. It got rid of the sense of exclusion felt by its acolytes. David had already considered this. They over-idealised themselves and gave themselves grand titles and pushed away people who wanted to become therapists, and it was all designed to ease the sense of not belonging to ordinary society. Its tenets weren't exactly routinely valued by medics or by the general public.

Later that month, however, a lift to his mood was brought about by a call from a psychotherapist he had approached with a view to a vacancy, who was offering to see him in the week before the holidays with the thought that a therapy could start after the break.

His first impression was a favourable one. This new therapist had a calm presence, but he was nevertheless warm, and engaged freely with what David had to say about what had brought him to therapy and there were no negative comments about the fact that this was now the third therapist he had consulted. His consulting room was one of several in a flat on the ground floor of a Victorian terraced house, and the furnishings were what David had come to expect: the Turkish rug on the floor, the huge numbers of books on shelves, side lamps on polished tables, and a number of plants, with a large and graceful palm clearly enjoying the light from the bow window. A red velvet coverlet lay over the couch and David, glancing at it, thought that it looked inviting. He laughed to himself at his immediate positive feeling, but he could not help taking to this man who, with his black hair turning to grey, was someone he felt he might be like in ten years' time. His comments during the consultation were reassuringly clear and understandable in terms of what was bringing David to seek help at this point, linking the failure to be accepted by the Radcliffe to his early experience as he had described it, and linking an anxiety about this to his possible anxiety about starting again with a new therapist who was himself from the Radcliffe. David felt that he was with someone who was accurately picking up and commenting on his state of mind at that moment: the swingeing sense of hurt at the way that he had been treated causing a grimness in his mind at the approach to each day; a depressing sense of déjà vu and of being blocked, which he could only bear with in the hope that his mood would lift. At least this man seemed to have an understanding of the way that the Radcliffe operated. There wasn't an immediate denial of the gravity of the impact of it on him. There was a willingness to entertain the possibility that the Radcliffe was not treating applicants appropriately; David could hardly believe his ears when he heard the term "abuse of power" being used as he described his experiences. Here was someone who wasn't blinded by an allegiance to an organisation that was prone to reject applicants for training apparently on a whim.

On the pavement again after the meeting, with a start to a therapy booked for after Easter, David felt reassured and comforted. This therapist, Alexander Darwin, seemed to him to represent a capacity for hopefulness that David was on the brink of losing. Could it be that he was related to *the* Darwin, the Charles Darwin of *On the Origin of Species*, the Darwin who had endured years travelling on the *Beagle*, with its attendant discomforts? David had just finished reading a biography written by John Bowlby, the eminent psychiatrist, and had been impressed by Darwin's comment that in fact it was his repeated illness that had created the space necessary for him to do the work on his famous book. David felt similarly that he was well physically, but that he had been psychologically affected by his earliest experiences, and in addition, the later difficulties in the family. He needed to think in terms of his internal state, which he had to acknowledge to himself was sometimes not of the best, as paving the way to his ability to engage empathetically with some very damaged people. Some of the therapists who had interviewed him clearly felt that his background was so negative in its influence on him that he could not possibly function as a psychotherapist; but others seemed to accept that this sort of background would provide the motivation for working in the field and would provide a rich seam to be mined in the interests of the development of a clinical working capacity.

# FOURTEEN

David hoped the new therapy would provide a setting in which he could encounter the thinking of the Spaltung set of therapists at the Radcliffe, as well as a place where he could recover from the shock of the interviews and his failure to be accepted. As spring progressed, he certainly felt a new liveliness; warmth was not only all around him but seemed to affect his state of mind, so that he noticed with pleasure the thickening buds on the trees and the sunlit white clouds, which seemed to bloom against the freshly blue sky. He didn't travel in the Easter break, contenting himself with being at home or doing some sailing with Jack and enjoying playing with the baby. For the summer holiday, however, he found himself planning a trip to visit a friend who had settled in Norway. With a pleasurable sense of anticipation he worked out a cheap route from Newcastle to Bergen by sea, and from there by steamer up the coast. His friend Roald would meet him at the small harbour and drive him to the family farm.

Sailing towards the Norwegian coast after a night on board was exciting; a new experience. The wind snatched at his hair and he was glad of his jacket as the boat plunged in the final approach to land, the tops of the waves being whipped off as spray, and the engine pushing steadily on. The creamy wake curved behind, and looking forward past white-painted metal stanchions David could see blue-grey mountains and white or rust-red painted houses dotted in unlikely rocky places all along the coast. Coming into Bergen was an excitement too, and finding the right steamer to take him further up the coast. The houses on the hillsides gradually became less frequent as they headed northwards, and three hours later, as the boat settled alongside a jetty in the still water of a mountainous fjord, David felt a long way from any urban landscape. The talk was all in Norwegian as people greeted friends and various items were unloaded from the boat along with the passengers. He saw Roald immediately, a stocky figure in corduroys, with straw-coloured hair. Roald's English was still good. They had worked together in David's first job as a clinical psychologist, and there was much news to catch up on as they drove on narrow roads up through the fells and then along innumerable valleys to the farm. Roald told David that he was staying with his family for the summer before taking up a new post in the autumn as a psychology lecturer at Oslo University. His parents would be glad of an extra pair of hands on the farm; they still dried the hay on racks on the hillsides rather than in a silo. David's help with this task would be invaluable.

At the farmhouse, set just outside a little town, Roald's parents and sister greeted him warmly. Fru Opdahl, Roald's mother, was a little woman, grey-haired and apple-cheeked, who hugged him warmly and said something in Norwegian, which Roald translated as her pleasure in seeing any friend of her son's but also a concern for him, wasn't he bringing a girlfriend or wife? Slightly embarrassed, David beamed a reply and was greeted by Herr Opdahl, a taller version of his wife, dressed in blue dungarees and worn shirt. Marta, Roald's sister, like him blonde and clear-eyed, smiled warmly and pressed his hand. David had met her once before when she had visited Roald in London, and she was at home on the farm, having settled for a rural life as the wife of a neighbouring farmer—the wedding would take place in the autumn. The farmhouse was on the side of a lake, with a huge mountain opposite. In the bright sky a few clouds scudded along just below the summit of the mountain, driven by the southerly wind. The hill behind the farmhouse led via a col to a higher mountain where patches of snow still lay despite the warm sunshine. The farmhouse was cosy; grey tiles on the roof, wooden veranda and walls, and wood everywhere indoors. David noticed through an open door that Roald's parent's room had a huge bed that seemed to be built rather like a box, with huge wooden bed-head and foot. He was shown to his room, at the front of the house, overlooking the lake and mountain. Rugs lay on the polished wooden floor and there was a wood-fired stove to provide heat. Light colours on the walls and furnishings provided a cheerful feel and David realised, looking at the bed, that he was very tired after all the travelling. He rested before joining the family at supper in the kitchen. The conversation proceeded in a mixture of Norwegian and English, Roald doing a parallel translation for the family.

That night he dreamt vividly, first about the travelling in which the boat seemed to plough endlessly towards a coast which never got any closer. Then he was walking in the mountains, and dimly far off he could see his mother waving, smiling to him. He woke with a start, still, in an involuntary way, trying to get across the hillside towards her. He realised that Roald was tapping at the door, asking him if he was ready for breakfast; the family would be starting work soon. He hurriedly shaved and dressed, going to the kitchen and enjoying a large breakfast of white bread, which Roald said Fru Opdahl made herself, with red jam of some sort, also home-made, and hot coffee, which smelt deliciously fragrant and steamed in the sunlight from the window. After breakfast he went out and helped with the back-breaking task of driving stakes into the ground in lines and running wire between them on which to hang the hay from the nearby fields. It was a sunny morning, but the ground was wet with dew and there was a real pleasure in picking up handfuls of sweet-smelling hay and hanging it on the racks of wire to dry.

The next few days passed in the same way, with a lot of hard work from the family in getting the hay harvest on to the racks while the sun shone in an almost cloudless sky. On the Saturday Roald suggested climbing the mountain behind the farmhouse and so he, Marta, and David set out after breakfast, carrying packed lunches. David was left struggling in the rear as the other two, long accustomed to climbing the hills, headed upwards with unrelenting speed. He was also hampered by his footwear, a pair of old trainers, which had worn smooth on the sole and were slippery on the grass. He wished he had brought his walking boots with him. They would have made the walking easier. As they gained height the view down into the valley and across to the mountain on the other side of the lake was stunningly beautiful. Roald pointed out to him, as they climbed higher, that it was just possible to see the edge of a glacier, a river of ice gleaming in the distance like a frozen presence, seemingly as solid as the dark rock and grey-green hillsides of the mountains that surrounded it.

At the top, looking down into the valley on the far side of the mountain, they rested and had lunch, eating the little blueberries that festooned the bushes. They lay down in the sun afterwards. Marta pointed at David's mouth and chin, laughing at the spreading blue stain from the berries.

"We can all see what you've been eating," she laughed at him in her sunny way.

"You're just as bad," he said, and couldn't help but admire her full lips stained blue and the way that her blue eyes seemed to echo the colour. He thought of Schubert's song-cycle,

"*Die schöne Müllerin*", and the miller's daughter with her eyes blue as forget-me-nots ... he realised that the sun was so warm he had become sleepy. That was probably why he was thinking such dreamy thoughts ... the deep musical notes from the bells around the necks of the mountain goats faded, and he slept for a while, the grass scratchy against his face, being tickled by little insects. He was woken by Roald.

"David!" There seemed to be a note of urgency in Roald's voice. "Are you awake? We should get off the mountain quite quickly, there is a storm coming ..." David looked in the direction he was pointing, and could see dark clouds forming above the glacier. The sky where they were was still bright and tranquil, and there was hardly a breeze to stir the heat-haze over the tops of the nearby mountains. He could not understand why there was still snow up here, patches of it looking old and crusted in the shady spots. They picked up their rucksacks and headed down over the tufts of stiff grass and past the patches of little blueberry bushes and rocks. Again, David struggled to keep up with Roald and Marta as the way began to be increasingly vertiginous.

As he leapt and half-ran down the steep slope he remembered Darwin's journal about his travels on the *Beagle*. His description of his trip into the mountains in Tahiti was vivid: his horror at the impossible steepness of the volcanic hills, and his sense of relief that the sheer drops were often concealed from his sight by the luxuriant tropical vegetation, leaves covering the narrow ridges where his guides had encouraged him to perch as they clambered out of a gorge on to the heights. David told himself to concentrate on where he was putting his feet. He was slipping alarmingly on the grassy patches in-between the rocks. Then he realised that they were approaching a particularly steep grass slope. There was only a narrow ledge at the bottom of it before a cliff plunged to the floor of the valley. Surely they hadn't come up this way.

His feet began to slide from under him. He was thinking that perhaps Roald and Marta had chosen this route as the most direct down from the tops. He realised that Roald had turned to look at him from ten feet below. His face registered concern. David began to slide, faster and faster down the grassy near-perpendicular slope.

"David! Dig your heels in!" cried Roald. There wasn't time to reply. David cannoned into Roald with the full force of his fall. Roald braced himself with his back against a spur of rock and David fell breathless at his feet. Roald picked him up and brushed him down.

"I said let's hurry down the mountain, not fall off it!" he said, patting David's back. "It's okay, I caught you." David grinned, breathless but trembling with the shock of so nearly having fallen over the cliff. He could imagine only too vividly how devastating a fall it would have been.

"Next time I'll bring my walking boots," he said.

"We'll go a bit slowly now," said Roald. And in fact it wasn't long before they were walking along the edge of the field with the hay-racks, the remnants of the sun soaking the racks with light and drawing out a sweet fragrance. As they arrived at the farmhouse the rain began to pelt down in large warm drops, and thunder began to crash back and forth amongst the mountains.

Fru Opdahl smiled as she saw their mouths stained with blueberries and their heightened colour from the run down the mountain. She said something to Roald and laughed. He turned to David.

"She says you look as though you have fallen down the mountain, not walked down it," he said and David laughed wryly.

"You can tell her that was almost what happened," he said. "But it's good that we hurried. We would have got soaked."

"Yes, and lightning isn't good on the tops of the mountains," said Roald.

The rain drummed on the roof while they ate supper. They turned to playing cards and it was a companionable cosy evening. Herr Opdahl lit the wood-stove in the living room and they talked long into the night. The following Saturday there was a traditional dance in the local village hall. The walls were decorated with freshly cut branches of silver birch and the smell of the foliage permeated the atmosphere. David enjoyed the traditional music to which the dancers swung and stamped. Walking home through the bright semi-gloom of the northern dusk with the sun seemingly only just below the horizon, Roald asked him what the future might hold for him, now that the Radcliffe had turned him down.

"I think you should protest," he said. "It's not right that they can encourage you to apply again and again, over years, literally years, offer you a training therapist—and then say that you don't have enough academic qualifications. What do they want—a professor?"

David laughed uncomfortably. He had not thought of protesting. He was worried that if he did he would be seen in a very negative light and to be humiliating himself in relation to the decision. He said something of this to Roald, but he did not get a sympathetic response.

"Go and see them with a lawyer," Roald said. "I would."

"A lawyer?" said David, rather shocked. "How would that help?"

"It would frighten them into behaving in a reasonable way. They have treated you abominably. You can't take this lying down."

And, while he was in fact lying down on his new therapist's couch, back again after the summer, David did begin to mull over the question of whether he should protest about what had happened to him. It did seem extraordinary that he should be encouraged to apply with the offer of help in finding a training therapist—and then be told to go away. He found himself talking about the lack of coherence in the way that he had been dealt with. Frank Darwin seemed fair about the Radcliffe, and wasn't prickly and biased in its favour in the way that his previous therapist had been. He did not hesitate to deal with the reality of the situation, as well as what it might represent in David's internal world, or in relation to the here-and-now of the sessions. Initially anxious about this new enterprise, David began to relax into the work of the therapy.

Not long after he had returned home after his break in Norway, he went as usual after work to his session, the crisp autumn sunshine picking out the shapes of the trees in the road in vivid detail; David was reminded of Klimt's paintings of trees dappled with light in a very similar way. A cat sat at the side of the road, grey with orange eyes that gleamed oddly at David as she glanced at him before carrying on with her dreaming in the sun. David thought of the dream he had woken from the night before, which was about cats. He looked forward to telling Alexander Darwin about it.

"I had a dream last night," he started the session. "It was about a group of cats. You know that phrase about trying to organise a group of people to do something, it was like trying to herd cats?" A grunted assent. "Well, in my dream I was writing a letter to the group at the Radcliffe, where they decide whether to accept people or not. But I knew that I was writing a letter to a group of cats!" Darwin laughed.

"You're not going to tell me that in your dream you thought the group were like a herd of cats!" he said, laughing. David laughed too. From where he was lying on the couch he could see the sky, and a eucalyptus tree standing still, exquisitely side-lit by the sun sinking to the west. He thought of the Clough poem in which the land was bright to the west; in fact he did feel more hopeful and bright, with this steady and easily amused presence benignly attending to his state of mind.

"Well, I *am* going to tell you that, actually! In my dream I was puzzled about what language to use in writing to a herd of cats—would they be able to read my letter? Or should I be sending them a taped message they could listen to ... and I imagined, in my dream, one cat reading the letter to the others and all of them not really attending, one of them eating a plate of sardines off the table, another licking its fur, another saying something about how inappropriate it was for cats to sit at a table. They were all different colours, but the same thing about all of them was the extent to which they were self-preoccupied ..." Darwin laughed again.

"So what happened in the end in your dream?"

"Well, I actually decided in the end to write a letter to the cats. I felt sure that it would be hopeless, but I thought I would do it anyway, and what I said was how I thought that the way I had been treated was so lacking in care, so incoherent ..."

There was a pause. David could hear the traffic outside the window, people beginning to go home from work. Somewhere, someone was whistling a tune that he couldn't identify.

"Well, what do you think about the dream, then?" Darwin said.

"I'm not sure, really. It could be to do with my anxiety about whether a letter of mine to the Radcliffe could ever be thought about in a sensible way ..."

"Yes, you don't have much experience of a mind functioning sensibly there, do you?" said Darwin drily. "Particularly one that attends to you."

There was another pause.

"I think you're right in your view of the dream. However, we could look at it as it relates to your expectations here, maybe … perhaps you have a worry that I won't be able to think about you properly, that I will be thinking inside myself about what you bring to your sessions, but it will be incoherent, a herding cats sort of mentality, as I discuss with myself my thinking about what you bring."

David laughed. "I can see that," he said. "My experience of therapy so far has been a bit like that. I had a very good experience with Dr Smythe. He was elderly, but incredibly experienced, and well able to deal with a situation like mine where there has been a lot of loss in reality; death and illness in the family … he was obviously thinking, working thoughtfully … and as for Sonya, she was just in her own world, linked in with the Radcliffe. She orbits around it like a tied planet, no independent thought of her own."

"Mmm. Pretty searing as a judgement. But perhaps these people, these other therapists—or cats—have a useful function; the heat's turned away from me."

"What do you mean?" asked David, puzzled.

"I mean that you might have all sorts of feelings about the fact that we just start on the therapy, and then I am off on my holiday travels—self-interested, you might feel …"

"Oh I don't think that at all. You're entitled to your breaks. I know—I know that's what I am supposed to think … it's all about what I feel about you, in the transference, you know?"

"Yes … the transference," said Darwin meditatively. "You don't think that these feelings I'm talking about, the feelings about being with a herd of cats who are completely wrapped up in themselves, so that you are ignored … you don't think that these feelings belong to a much younger side of you … it's those feelings I am talking about, which maybe your dream refers to?"

It was David's turn to reflect on what Darwin was saying. He could see it; it was an obvious link to make—the selfish cats at the Radcliffe, his feelings of being neglected in his earliest infant moments in the incubator in the hospital, or being neglected in favour of his sisters, or in his father's decline into a depression.

"Well, I can see what you mean. I bring the feelings about my earliest experiences into the session. But of course there is a reality about the way the Radcliffe behaved."

"I'm not disputing that. And in that way, your dream, amusingly enough, paints a picture of how you have experienced all the different interviews you had there."

Later, at home in his flat, David thought that he should make a statement about the way he had been treated. He thought it very likely that if he made a complaint, it would be taken seriously and acted upon. His idealising notion of a response to his complaint was that he would be listened to carefully, and that he might then be accepted after all. Hadn't Coulterden said that they might well have made a mistake in his case? He would write, and it would all be sorted out. The people who had written him references, and Jack and Clara—they all felt he was suitable. They all professed amazement that he had been turned down, but without exception they had also remarked that it was very common for applicants to be turned down on the slightest pretext. He thought he would ring Clara. He hadn't spoken to her since he had got back from Norway, but her postcard to him from Corsica took centre stage on his kitchen counter, where his eye fell on it each morning with a frisson of pleasure at the thought that she had been thinking of him while she was away. Admittedly she was away with Georg, but ... could it be that they had chosen to visit Corsica because he had told her about his trip there? He liked the idea that this might be the case, smiling down at the postcard.

He rang her. Clara seemed pleased to hear from him. He told her about his trip. She said that hers had been interesting, but it had been far too hot. They had travelled inland, to visit Corte, the town in the heart of the island at the foot of Monte Cinto, the 6,000-foot mountain at the centre of Corsica, and she told him about their trip halfway to the top, the refreshing coolness of the river they had followed, how clear it was and how much she had enjoyed basking in the sun with her feet in the cold water. He enjoyed her traveller's tales and was interested in the fact that at this time of the evening one might have expected her to be eating supper with Georg, but there was not a hint of hurry in her manner, no desire to get him off the phone quickly while she attended to domestic matters. Finally, he could not resist asking her how Georg was. Her tone hardened slightly.

"He's out, actually," she said. "At a meeting at the Radcliffe."

"There's so much evening work, isn't there, in the psycho-therapy organisations, the Radcliffe's no different, I suppose," he said. "Well, to tell the truth," and her tone became confiding, "there's a lot of work at the moment because the Radcliffe is in difficulties."

"Difficulties?" he said a little incredulous. How could such an august body (even if inhabited by felines, he laughed inwardly, and made a mental note to tell her of his dream), how could such a body be in difficulties?

"Yes ... they're having difficulty in attracting people to train, and having difficulty in finding patients for people to act as their training patients. People don't have the time or the money nowadays to come to therapy sessions three days a week ... I'm sure that half the people at the Radcliffe have a practise made up of people who are themselves training in the psychotherapy organisations ..."

"I should think you're right." He had heard similar sorts of worries being expressed by psychotherapy colleagues in the building where he had his consulting room. But Clara seemed to feel she had said too much, and quickly asked him about his failed application, how did he see things developing?

"I think—and I'd like to see what you think—I'm going to complain. You know Roald, the friend I went to stay with in

Norway? He was very insistent that I should take it up with them, the way that I've been treated."

Clara sounded dubious. "Do you think it's worth it? Don't you think they'll just push you away?"

"Well, the logic of it would be, if they're having difficulty in recruiting now, to look more kindly on applicants."

"Yes—you would think that, wouldn't you? That's the obvious course of action. The trouble is, they're a very mixed group of people. Pushing decisions through is very difficult. If two people have one view, you can guarantee that two others will have a completely different view." He agreed with her inwardly. The way he had been dealt with communicated the disparity of views very clearly. Perhaps he wouldn't tell her his cat dream—he didn't want to offend her by seeming too negative about the place where, after all, she was going to lodge herself professionally. That thought prompted another question from him.

"Are you going to move into private practice full time when you finish your training, then?" he asked her and this led to a discussion between the two of them about ways of conducting a psychotherapeutic career, private practice versus the NHS or public sector and so on. Finally it was David who said he had to make a move, prepare some things for the next day.

He went to bed that night pleased with his sense that Clara seemed very open to approaches from him, and in fact he dreamt that night, not of cats, but of himself and Clara, swimming in a warm, clear Mediterranean sea ... and was woken by his alarm clock to a pleasurable sense of renewed possibilities where she was concerned. As he ate his toast and marmalade and contemplated the sunshine beginning to warm the top of the kitchen window he reflected that he had spent the hour talking to Clara that he might have spent in writing to the Radcliffe. He wondered if this was significant. One of his supervisors, an elderly woman psychotherapist whose husband had died during the course of the long period of time he had been supervised by her, had said after his death that she wished she had spent more time with him, and less at the Radcliffe. People mistake therapy for real life, she had said. Was he in danger of doing the same thing, preoccupied as he was, and had been, with the progress of his application for psychotherapy training?

FIFTEEN

D avid did send in a complaint. To his chagrin, he was passed from pillar to post, with lengthy delays. He wrote first to the group that dealt with applications, on the basis that he had been told at his last set of interviews that his academic qualifications were not sufficient and that he should have been told this before he had put in a long series of applications lasting years. A long delay ensued, after which he received a letter suggesting that he had no cause for complaint and that he should let the matter drop. He then wrote to the group responsible for the education of psychotherapists. After the passage of several months, he was brushed off in the same way. He wrote to the director, and was invited to a meeting with him. The meeting at least gave him a chance to air his concerns, but once again he was brushed aside, with the thought offered that perhaps he was harbouring a grievance. He protested at this pathologising of what seemed to him a legitimate matter of concern, but to no avail.

Autumn had turned into spring and into autumn again before he got to the point of making a complaint to the group in charge of ethics. His argument was that it could not be ethical to suggest that he was, at his third application, not sufficiently qualified to train as a psychotherapist. A further complaint was

Coulterden's handling of his interview in which he was given the impression that Coulterden's mind was already made up.

With the group in charge of ethics, he began to feel a shift in the ground. He met one of its members, Margaret Fortescue, at her private consulting room and felt that he was listened to with concern and empathy. This was followed by a telephone call from another elderly woman therapist who asked him what it was he wanted in making this complaint, how could it be taken forward? He explained that he wanted to be given another chance to apply on the basis that he had not been dealt properly with at his third set of interviews.

In January David was invited to meet with two of the members of the committee in charge of ethics: Margaret Fortescue, again, and Donna-Mae Shute. He arrived at the door of the Radcliffe, only to find that he could not work out how to get into the building, the door having no obvious bell or way of announcing his presence. Had he been less nervous about the meeting he would have thought this appropriate, symbolic of the "no entry" stance of the place. To him, at least. After a few minutes of puzzled attempts to get in he was followed to the door by Margaret Fortescue, who greeted him kindly and showed him in. She had a key to the door, David noted. He was taken upstairs to a room with a large table at which sat Donna-Mae Shute, the elderly woman therapist whom he had spoken to on the phone. She was a white-haired American woman with a warm smile. To one side was a tall window casting a bright light.

Invited to join them at the table he was offered a glass of water, which he accepted. He was then asked if he would like the meeting minuted. He was bewildered by this offer. Why would he want the meeting minuted? He declined, wondering if he was doing the right thing, but it really didn't seem necessary. Donna-Mae Shute started the interview by saying that Margaret

Fortescue had explained the substance of his concern to her, so that she was up-to-date on what were the main issues.

"We have no concerns about the way that you were interviewed," she said.

"No concerns?" said David. "Do you mean to say that you're not concerned about the fact that someone who's been interviewed twice before and has been offered help in finding a training psychotherapist, should be told at the latest set of interviews that they aren't suitable by reason of the fact that they haven't sufficient academic qualifications?"

Anna-Mae Shute looked nonplussed and looked at her colleague for guidance. She cleared her throat, but said nothing. Finally Anna-Mae Shute answered.

"You need to take that issue to the group that deals with the education of therapists," she said.

"I did that," said David flatly. "I was told that there wasn't a concern. That's the reason I am bringing this issue to this group. It can't be ethical to change the goalposts in this way, and suddenly tell an applicant that they're somehow not qualified enough."

"Well, I don't know about that," said Anna-Mae Shute. "The fact of the matter is that we have talked to some people, and the feeling is that you aren't suitable to train."

"What people?" said David. "Who have you talked to?"

"I'm not really at liberty to say," said Anna-Mae Shute. "An additional matter is that all the people who interviewed you thought that it wouldn't be in your best interests to allow you to train."

"But then why was I offered help in finding a training therapist?"

"I can't comment on that," said Anna-Mae Shute.

"It does seem to suggest that the view taken of my application wasn't as clear-cut as you're implying. And anyway, I'm not making a complaint about not being accepted. I *am* making a complaint about my academic qualifications now being regarded as insufficient."

There was a pause. David sipped at his water. He began again, carefully, although he knew clearly now that he wasn't going to get anywhere in this atmosphere of negativity towards him.

"I really think that you should be taking what I am complaining about seriously," he said.

"You must be very angry to have been turned down," said Margaret Fortescue. She was a stocky woman and under pressure she was beginning to look rather florid.

"Yes, you can talk about my state of mind," said David. "But it wouldn't be appropriate, since this isn't a clinical setting."

"Ah, but you're turning it into one," said Margaret Fortescue quickly. "You have been told in a variety of different ways that you aren't suitable to train as a therapist, but you don't take it in."

"That's because I don't agree with this assessment of my capacities," said David. "And at any rate, it shouldn't be a decision of the group dealing with ethics to decide whether I'm suitable as an applicant or not. Surely your decision ought to be about whether I was dealt with properly."

Margaret Fortescue tutted irritably. "The trouble with you is, you just don't listen. You were dealt with properly. Andrew Coulterden spelt it out for you. You had a follow-up interview with him. You just don't listen."

"Indeed I do listen," said David with some heat but a resigned feeling that he was wasting his time. "And what I'm hearing is that there isn't a chance of what I am saying about my interviews and the fairness of the application process being taken seriously. I have explained that it was clear that Andrew Coulterden had already made his mind up. And so have these people you have spoken to. I can see I am wasting my time here." With that he stood up and walked out.

On the pavement David fumed. Why hadn't he followed Roald's suggestion, and taken a lawyer with him? Or perhaps he should have asked Jack to come with him. But this was impossible: for Jack to be seen to be siding with someone who was making a complaint would have been risky for the development of his career. He would not be thought kindly of if he were seen to be supporting someone who was thought of as a nuisance. David walked away from the Radcliffe.

Recounting the experience to his therapist later that day he realised that he had no further wish to take things forward. No further way forward for them, either, since his complaint. He remembered all the people he knew who had also unaccountably been turned down, to the mystification of their friends and colleagues. Later in the week, as he began to work through the matter in his therapy, he began to understand the set dynamics a little better. He felt more definitely that he was being made to carry feelings of exclusion that more properly belonged to an institution excluded from the ordinary life of society. Occasionally, a psychotherapist who was an academic might get public recognition, but it was a cloistered world. No system of checks and balances to ensure that people like Coulterden were encouraged to treat applicants fairly. In fact, later, David was to hear that he had been removed from his post as chair of the group that interviewed applicants. He did not belong to the Spaltung set, and was found to be routinely pushing away applicants who were with Spaltung set therapists, because he disapproved of the set's thinking so much. Since the interviewing was done behind closed doors, it had been a long time before this was noticed … David wondered what was going to be done about those hopeful young applicants, turned down because they were with the wrong sort of psychotherapist. He knew the answer to that question: nothing.

# SIXTEEN

It was a relief to David that he was with a therapist who was clearly appalled at the way he had been treated. He could hold on to a sense of the competence of some therapists, even though the institution itself was, as he put it to himself, in trouble. He could clearly differentiate between what belonged to the dynamics of the Radcliffe and how his own internal world might be linked with those dynamics and throw up a mesh to ensnare him, potentially, into misery. Gradually recovering a degree of objectivity about what he had been through—in his attempts to be accepted by what he could now think of as an impressive organisation but one in some difficulty—he could get on with his life. He could attend to his own patients, his work with the families—and his pursuit of Clara. It was a significant problem that Clara had come to the end of her training at the Radcliffe and was becoming involved there … but she was none the less desirable for that. If only Georg wasn't there … and, he could see, Georg was increasingly not there. He and Clara often talked on the phone in the evenings now, and she was the first to learn of his thought that he would visit Alaska in the summer, that it would do him good to travel, to get away from his routine and the Radcliffe. He would have a trip; he would visit his friend Gemma Stadtler in Alaska; he would return in September invigorated. He could see that Clara was rather regretful that she could not accompany him. Her projected trip in summer with Georg to his family, followed by walking in the Alps, clearly didn't seem so attractive to her, and he sensed that the relationship was in difficulties. But it was still a relationship, and there was no point in trying to hasten the decline of it in too obvious a way. He told Clara about Gemma, and she was politely interested, trying, he felt, to push away jealous feelings about this other woman.

"I met Gemma when she was studying as a child psychotherapist at the Limes clinic. She's a thoughtful person—has done academic work in the socio-cultural field and managed to train as an analyst in the States."

"I thought only medics could train as analysts in the States," Clara objected as they sat over a glass of wine in his flat. "Or maybe that's the way it used to be—it's different now." The roses were out, brightly, in the garden, and a cat was keeping an eye on the birds that were fluttering in the bushes.

"You would have thought that, wouldn't you? But in fact—she was a sociology academic so she trained on that basis." Clara frowned.

"Is she in a relationship?"

"No, I don't think so. She's very involved in wildlife photography in Alaska."

"Exotic!" said Clara with a slightly pettish look, and fretfully flicked the base of her wine glass with a fingernail. "You know, you being turned down by the Radcliffe ... such a shame." David didn't think until afterwards that her change of subject was designed to obscure from herself her jealous feeling about Gemma. He felt a wave of irritation and at the same time a sort of glumness. She was alright, she was trained now—could afford to be rather grandiose. For the first time in their relationship he found himself being sharp with her.

"It is a shame, being turned down … but it's more than that, it's an injustice. Should've taken a lawyer with me to the meeting."

"Why's that?" said Clara. "What good would a lawyer have done?"

"Well, they wouldn't have been so rude if a lawyer had been present, a witness to their behaviour. The trouble is there are no checks and balances, it all happens behind closed doors—though"—he was able to chuckle at this—"they did offer me the opportunity to have the meeting recorded. I should've been suspicious when they offered that, rather than being so trusting. Naive, even. Organisations close ranks in a situation like this, don't they?"

"Well, David, all I can say is that it is a shame, a pity," she sighed and he felt a distinct sense that her glance contained a hint of schadenfreude, which annoyed him again.

"All very well for you to be sympathetic … you're alright, aren't you? You've trained … not that I can now expect you to be active in dealing with the dynamics at the Radcliffe—the ones that lead to perfectly good applicants being turned down."

"But I've only been there five minutes! What do you expect me to do in that time?"

She was nettled by his remark. He observed the colour in her face change, the lips compress. But he didn't expect the venomous outburst that followed.

"You always think other people are better off than you! There's a word for it: self-pitying, I think that's the right one. Hasn't it occurred to you that you might simply not have been acceptable on the basis of your capacity as a clinician—or your academic status?" She had struck on the one thing that was surely going to wound him. He was proud of his academic record … had indeed thought of pursuing an academic career.

"What nonsense! My academic credentials are quite impressive—I know I haven't written many papers …"

"No, you haven't!" she interrupted. "You've not written much. They would be aware of that. They might've been concerned about how much you would contribute to the life of the Radcliffe, the academic life, I mean. They might've thought, not much!"

He was horrified. How had it come to this, that they were at odds with each other? The light was going from the sky, the birds had fallen quiet. There was momentary silence between them as they glared at each other. Then Clara leapt to her feet, grabbing her bag and muttering something about needing to get home, closing the door behind her with something of a bang.

David ran the conversation over in his mind through the rest of that solitary evening. He found himself at the computer, emailing friends, firming up with Gemma his trip in the summer. He went to bed sick at heart, convinced that matters with Clara were not going to go any further, despite his best hopes. At work the next day, he found it difficult to concentrate in the team meeting. There were worried discussions going on there too, about resourcing. Destructive lack of staffing, he commented to himself as the child psychiatrist and the principal child psychotherapist were trying to put in a bid for more funding. He found himself trying to step in to help as best he could as they struggled with the task. The team meetings took place in the psychiatrist's room, which was the largest in the building, and normally he found the setting enjoyable, liking the view into the garden and glad of the fact that there was a respite in the meeting from the intensity of the clinical encounters that took up the rest of the days. However, today he could hardly focus on the discussion.

He was equally preoccupied when he went to see his patients in his consulting room. Hugh was making good progress, but David was concerned about the impact on him of the two-month summer break he was planning for the summer. He had given his patients the dates and had cleared with work that he would take some unpaid leave to allow him the time off. He had inherited a small sum of money from his aunt, which would help with the finances.

June was hot that year and as usual his consulting room was overly warm, so that he needed to draw the curtains to shield himself and his patients from the worst of the heat. He had told Hugh about the break, and to his consternation Hugh uncharacteristically didn't seem to find anything unusual in the impending lengthy absence of his counsellor.

Hugh had brought a dream. Again, this was uncharacteristic, and David felt some relief as Hugh began to describe the dream, feeling that this might be the route through which it might be possible to help Hugh process his feelings about the long break.

"I was in Alaska," said Hugh. He paused for thought. David was momentarily confused. Did he mean that he had actually been to Alaska? And what a coincidence, that he himself was going to Alaska shortly.

"Is this in the dream?" he asked eventually, after the silence had become rather prolonged. He was beginning to feel sleepy in the warmth of the room.

"Yes, that's right," said Hugh. He sighed, shifted around. "It's very hot in here today. Could you put the fan on?"

"Alright." David stood up, put the fan on maximum output, and set it so that it oscillated from side to side. "Is that better?"

"Yes, it is. Thank you. In my dream I was in Alaska." There was another pause. David felt curious. Why was it taking Hugh so long to tell him the dream? He waited. Hugh's phone rang in his pocket. Hugh started, reached down and switched it off.

"Sorry," Hugh said. "They can call back later, whoever it was. Or perhaps they left a message. I'm waiting for work to call about an issue I hadn't quite finished. So, my dream last night. It was a very disturbing dream. I think I must have had it because I was too hot, it gets very hot indeed in my flat in this heat, the walls seem to hold the heat of the day and it's still hot at night." David resisted the temptation to ask him directly about his dream, interested to see whether Hugh would eventually tell him or not.

"The dream was about being attacked by a bear," said Hugh. "You know how bears hang about rivers in Alaska to catch salmon when they start to swim upstream?"

"Yes."

"Well, in my dream, I was in a river, a very cool river, I was swimming against the current, making some headway but not much. The water was beautifully clear, and looking down I could see the pebbles at the bottom of the river, and there seemed to be salmon in it, all swimming the same way as me. Then I looked up at the top of the waterfall and there was a really big black bear. I was terrified. I could see its black eyes glaring at me. It had huge paws with long sharp claws. It had seen me. It was beginning to scramble down the waterfall to get me when I woke up. I was in a real panic, it was such a relief when the dream wasn't actually real." He shuddered visibly.

"That was a very vivid dream, and it sounds quite terrifying," said David, thinking rapidly.

Would it make sense to Hugh if he linked it with his feelings about the break? He decided to see if Hugh had any ideas about the possible meaning of the dream.

"Why did you think you had such a frightening dream? What was it about, I wonder?" He thought that Hugh was beginning to understand how he might approach dreams, but on this occasion there was a stone wall. Hugh shifted uncomfortably again and said he had no idea what the dream might be about.

"Well, look," said David slowly. "What we have between us is a situation where I am providing you with a setting that you can swim in, so to speak. You're swimming, a bit like a salmon, back to your earliest roots. It seems to be a comfortable place for you to be in.

Cool water, very clear. You feel supported by the water, can see down through it to the pebbles at the bottom of the river. You are making progress, but feel it's slow. Then suddenly there is this awful presence, a huge bear."

Hugh shuddered again. David paused, and waited for him to speak, but there was silence so he went on. "Do you think that the bear in your dream might be to do with the anxiety you feel about the anger, the anger that part of you might feel, that really wants to attack me for having an unusually long break this year?"

"Oh God!" said Hugh, groaning dramatically. "You don't mean to tell me that you've found a way of making my dream, which, I might point out, was actually about me, as being about you? Why does everything I dream about or think about, have to be about you?" He almost sneered. "It's called narcissism, isn't it? It's got to be focused on you?"

David began to feel irritated, and he carefully did his best to remain calm. Had he been guilty of making a comment that was too far from Hugh's own experience? He silently mulled this over, and then Hugh put more pressure on him.

"Why are you taking such a long break this year, anyway? Normally you only take four weeks in the summer. Maybe you're taking a trip. Maybe you're the one going to Alaska. I do hope that a bear searches you out and decides you would make a good meal!" Unexpectedly Hugh laughed, clearly feeling that he was verging on being rather ridiculous.

David laughed too. It was quite an extraordinary link between them—Hugh had picked up so accurately that he was going to Alaska. And that in fact he was quite worried about the bear risk. He knew from Gemma's stories that she liked to get out into the wilderness and they had already started a dialogue about what sort of kit he would need to bring with him.

"You're turning it into a bit of a joke," David said. "And at an adult level you can quite appreciate that I do take breaks, wonder about what I am doing and so on. But maybe at a level that we often speak of, the level of a small child who feels abandoned, you do feel a real rage, an anger that eats away at you fiercely, and scares you."

Hugh could appreciate this, and David felt that he was with a patient who was prepared to be flexible, and think about what he offered in terms of comment.

He could not say the same about Clara; flexibility was obviously not one of her strengths. Or at least, that was what he told himself, when for the next week his phone calls went unanswered. Georg answered the phone once too often for his liking. Eventually he resorted to waiting for her one evening outside the clinic where she worked. She almost went to walk past him, face grimly set, looking straight ahead as she headed for her car, but she relented at the last minute and said a brief hello and something about going on to see patients at her consulting room just now, she didn't have time to talk.

"Well, come and have a coffee when you're finished," David urged, and reluctantly she agreed. It was a relief, later, to see her and to sit outside a café in the June warmth, sipping drinks and restored to some sort of communication. He realised that he had missed his choir practice—but he would do some practice by himself later. On impulse he asked her if she and Georg would like to come to the concert they were giving in two weeks. Her eyes clouded and she said that Georg would be away.

"Going to Switzerland?" asked David, and she nodded reluctantly. "Well come by yourself then. There'll be a glass of wine in the interval—it's Purcell—do you like Purcell?" And they were off into the musical preferences they each had. It was as if the argument hadn't happened.

Her presence at the concert, in the coolness of the church where the choir performed, sang in his mind like an anthem all of its own. Usually Rachel, standing in front of him in the sopranos, was there but she was absent, on a business trip. Delightfully, there was no impediment to meeting Clara in the interval and a sense of mutual warmth lit up her face. He hadn't seen her look so happy and relaxed for a while, and he was even immune to any competitive thought about this being a result of her having finished at the Radcliffe and having qualified as a psychotherapist. He was content to think that she was looking flushed and animated as a result of his presence. After the concert they walked back to his flat, which was nearby, and he could see that she was reluctant, after a lively discussion about music, to return to her own flat. They were due to see each other at Jack's house the following weekend for dinner, and David felt he could manage the sight of Clara with Georg with equanimity, now feeling clearer in his mind that she was attracted to him.

He arrived early at Jack and Marie's to help with preparations. Jack was in the kitchen, drinking a glass of wine and preparing salads, while Marie was sequestered upstairs dealing with childcare.

"Wine?" Jack asked. "Would you just get out the olives and crisps and put them on those plates there?" The kitchen was warmly done up with coloured wall tiles in earthy colours, a trio of lights hanging down in fluted glass lampshades over the long kitchen table where they were all to eat. It was a large room, serving partly as a living space, a room where Marie could be while Jack was seeing his patients in the front room. There was a squashy sofa in muted colours that echoed the colours of the tiles. At the back of the room, large French windows looked on to the garden in which roses sprawled over the lawn. Children's toys lay about, and the evening light gave a lustrous sheen to the surface of the water in a small pond. Once again David was impressed by the setting that Marie had created; he knew Jack could have lived in a garden shed, surrounded by shelves, without really noticing, so it must be all Marie's creativity that had gone into the pleasant surroundings.

"So, have you got over the meeting with the ethics group?" Jack asked him.

"Oh, I suppose so." David turned olives out of the jar he had been given into an earthenware dish with something of an irritable splat. He wasn't sure about Jack cutting to the chase, going directly for what was on his mind so much at the moment. But he realised that other guests would be arriving soon, and perhaps this accounted for the directness of Jack's enquiry. "It does seem so odd that the Radcliffe accepts some people, but not others, in such an arbitrary way. And as for Coulterden turning away applicants with Spaltung group therapists!"

Jack laughed, shaking the vinegar and oil together vigorously and reaching for garlic cloves and the garlic press.

"I'll let you into a secret," he said. "The director has set up a new group to look at the process of getting people in to train as therapists. There has been a lot of disquiet at precisely what you say—people being turned down in an arbitrary way. The group discussing applications in this way needs a bit of fine tuning. It's viewed now as needing some thought, how to mull over possible trainees and arrive at difficult decisions. Of course, you have to be sure that people are competent, and sound …"

In spite of himself, David was curious.

"What's brought this change about, then?" he asked. "It's apparently been going on for so long … I can remember talking to people ten years ago who were very wounded after being turned down, feeling their professional development had been blocked, their lives affected … especially when one partner in a marriage is accepted and the other not for some reason …" Jack made a small grunt of assent.

"Well, that's it precisely. Of course, the atmosphere is changing … ten years ago the Radcliffe was overwhelmed with good people wanting to train, it was very competitive. But the situation now is that there is less demand for three-times-a week therapy. People don't have the money, they don't have the time. Fewer patients, fewer people wanting to train. The existing therapists getting older, fewer young people coming into the profession … I wouldn't be surprised if they didn't revisit the applications of those people already turned down, invite people to reapply …"

"Oh, yes—just so that they can be treated badly all over again!" laughed David. "Catch me going anywhere near the Radcliffe now!" Jack didn't laugh. He looked serious.

"Well, that's the salad done," he said. "Now for the fruit salad. Just pass me the fruit bowl and I'll get the mangoes peeled and sliced. You know, David, I wouldn't be so dismissive. You're obviously someone with clinical capacity. I'm not the only one who thinks so. And it's such a waste, to lose good people like this. The atmosphere really is changing, you know. They're going to start up a scheme to encourage people who might think of training … introductory courses, all sorts of things." He glanced at David, fair hair gleaming in the light from the pendant lamps. "Don't say goodbye to the Radcliffe just yet."

There was a silence. He could hear the sparrows cheeping in the garden, a neighbour's children playing in a garden nearby. A plane went over, and David thought with relief of his imminent trip. He wanted to get away from all this; his patients, the families he saw at work, all this talk of the Radcliffe. He felt exhausted by it all. The doorbell rang.

"I'll get it, shall I?" he said, and walked to the front door, opening it to be greeted by Clara looking slightly uneasy, with Georg standing behind her proffering a bottle of wine.

"Hello, David," said Georg. "Shall I give Jack the wine?" He marched through to the kitchen where he and Jack were soon deep in Radcliffe gossip. David hadn't seen him for some time and found his manner more pleasant than last time they had met. Or, oddly enough, was it that he liked the presence of anyone, like Georg, who was linked to Clara in such an intimate way? Now that he himself was feeling closer to her? It was a change.

"Hello Clara," he said, kissing her on both cheeks. He could smell the sweetness of her perfume and she smiled warmly at him. She was fetchingly dressed in a tropical print outfit, the red in the design picked out with red shoes and green and red earrings. "You're looking wonderful," he couldn't resist adding. She smiled.

"I've brought a pudding," she said, and looking down David could see she was holding a glass bowl of meringue with cherries, strawberries, and blueberries.

"Lovely," he said automatically, taking it from her in such a way that their hands touched momentarily. He thought she too was not immune from the hypersensitivity to touch that he was feeling, and he was comforted by that. "Shall I get you some wine?" But here was Marie, coming down the stairs and greeting them both, taking them through to the kitchen and organising drinks and getting them settled on the sofas and chairs. Another person arrived, someone Marie and David both knew from the choir, who settled herself beside David and talked to him about his impending trip to Alaska. Soon another couple arrived, both recently qualified at the Radcliffe, contemporaries and friends of Jack's— Andrew, a pale man with a rather fishlike face and light-brown hair, another psychologist by background, and his wife, Uma, a vibrant Asian woman with long straight hair who lit up the room with her lively chat.

David was interested to hear from them about the developments at the Radcliffe. There were definitely changes afoot, and it was generally regarded that it was his bad luck to have been interviewed when he had been. Apart from Georg, that is, who annoyed David by pronouncing in oracular fashion that there must have been some anxiety about him.

"Then it would be understandable that you were turned down," he said. David changed the subject hastily, not liking the fact that his recent failure was under such public discussion, and likely to be commented on further by Georg. Did he sense, David wondered, not without some satisfaction, that he and Clara had a special intimacy? It was good to find that Andrew had spent some time in Alaska, trekking and travelling generally, and was prepared to go into detail about his trip.

"Yes, the bears," he said. "I did feel uneasy about them. But the important thing about Alaska is that it's generally understood that you mustn't feed them. I heard of a wildlife photographer who was killed by one by a river in the mountains after some people had been feeding bears … they come to associate humans with food, you see." Delightfully, David was aware of Clara looking anxious.

"But how do people keep themselves safe from bears if they're camping out and so on?" she asked, slightly tremulous.

"Well, I was travelling with a guide who had bear spray, a sort of pepper spray which stops them in their tracks. And you just have to be very careful … we never actually had to use it, though there was one occasion when we came across a bear with her cubs, quite by accident. But we stood still, made ourselves as unthreatening as possible and she just turned tail and ran."

"Do you plan to go back?" asked David and Uma answered, laughing, for them both.

"No, we're going to Italy this summer. It'll be hot—but no bears!"

Andrew and David chatted, and the evening passed pleasantly, in so far as it could for David when he had to endure Georg expounding—knowledgeably, he had to admit—on a particularly abstruse point of clinical work, as well as proprietorially patting Clara's hand from time to time. It seemed that he was trying to lay claim to Clara, as well as to the role of experienced clinician. It gave David a certain amount of pleasure to ask Clara about her cat, and to refer to his rescuing it, in front of Georg. He knew he was being childishly competitive, but her response was warm and direct and he had no sense that she disliked him for raising a matter of mutual interest that necessarily excluded Georg. It was also important to explain in her hearing that he was travelling with a friend in Alaska, someone who was an academic, an analyst, a child psychotherapist, a wildlife photographer—and a gay woman. He couldn't resist glancing at Clara when he gave this information to the dining table at large, but she evaded his look, and he could not tell what her reaction was as she looked neutrally at the table and sipped her wine.

# SEVENTEEN

As the little plane dipped down towards the inlet, David was entranced by the view. They seemed to be flying over a rainbow, which had its foot in dappled grey water, half lit by bright westering sun and half swathed in a veil of grey rain falling from a heavy black cloud. In another minute they were into the cloud and visibility was lost. He looked at Gemma. She was a tall woman, blond hair swept back behind her ears and green eyes lighting up a tanned face. She grinned at him and said, confidently, that the pilot of the plane had done this run hundreds of times before. The plane bounced slightly on landing, but it was smoothly done, and as David climbed from the plane and set about the business of helping unload their baggage he was relieved that the serious travelling was over. He felt jet-lagged and rather unlike himself after the long journey from London.

To be in Alaska and about to set out with Gemma on a camping trip was an excitement, and he looked about him eagerly. The little landing strip was adjacent to a small group of timber houses arranged in a strip on both sides of a rutted road, and he found it difficult to believe that the place was important enough to warrant it, but Gemma assured him that it was common, during the light summer months, for planes to fly in equipment, hikers, and photographers to this isolated spot. He was stunned by the tall mountains that ran down to the sea, their bases swathed in heavy forest, and snow still on their peaks. In the waters of the inlet were half a dozen boats, some of them clearly for fishing, others looking as though they were ready for taking trips up the coast.

Gemma and David were the only passengers on the plane and it was easy for their guide to spot them and come over, giving Gemma a hug and congratulating her on how well she looked.

"After the term I've had! I'm glad to leave it all behind," she said, disentangling herself from the bear-like hug and turning to introduce David.

"Glad to meet you," beamed Ed. He was a florid man, tall, his face crinkled and weather-beaten, wearing blue dungarees and a check shirt. His baseball cap covered greying cropped hair. "First time in Alaska?"

"Yes. It was a long trip getting here."

"Yeah, we're a long way from what you'd call civilisation here, right enough," Ed grunted as he helped them carry their gear into the bar of what seemed to be a very small hotel, built of clapboard covered in peeling white paint. "That road, see where it goes?" he pointed and David could see the road meandering up the side of the inlet. "Well, it goes on for another ten kilometres, alongside the coast, and then it just stops. After that, no people, no towns or roads, for a couple hundred miles. Just mountains, forests, sea. Lots of wildlife for people to see and photograph."

The hotel owner sorted some rooms for them and they met again in the bar where Ed stood them both a drink. "Supper later," he said, and winked at Gemma. "Still like salmon?" She laughed and said she did, especially done how the hotel cooked it. The bar was a small room congested with rickety tables and chairs and a few of the local people looked at them curiously. Ed addressed the room at large. "We're going up the coast for a while in the boat, then we're going to camp alongside the river," he said. "She's a great photographer, should get some good pictures. Salmon still running in the rivers, lots of bears."

"Yeah, we had one here right in the town last week," said a tanned elderly man who looked rather bear-like himself. "He ran off soon enough when we made a bit of noise."

Ed looked serious.

"That's the trouble with bears near here," he said. "They've come to link humans with food, and that's a bit risky."

"That's certainly the problem," said the hotel owner. "They were getting too interested in the town bins, but now the salmon are in the rivers they'll have plenty to get fat on."

David seriously hoped this was the case. He admitted to himself that this was the one element of the trip that he was finding concerning. It wasn't only his patient Hugh taking safety seriously in the presence of bears. As they loaded Ed's boat the following morning he was relieved to see that Ed had bear-spray canisters tucked in amongst the rest of the luggage. The boat was bobbing and bumping at its moorings as though keen to get going on the trip, and the sun sparkled on the water with such a glare that David was glad of his peaked cap and sunglasses. It took quite a few trips in the little dinghy, which the boat would tow behind it, to load all the provisions, the tents, the collapsible kayak for crossing rivers, the food, the cameras. A couple of men lounged and chatted with them as they dealt with the business of loading up. David felt doubtful that all their stuff could be stowed aboard Ed's boat but it was surprisingly capacious, and it wasn't long before all was packed and they could begin their trip, heading out of the inlet. The sea was choppy, dark blue waves being teased into white spray by a brisk wind. The sun shone from a bright sky and the sea birds were crying all around them, flung up into the air like bursts

171

of spray themselves, their wings tilted to the wind. David felt a burst of exhilaration as they chugged steadily away from the little settlement. The wind was behind them and they seemed to be passing an endless succession of skerries and little inlets quite quickly. The forested hillsides rose steeply above the inlets towards the high mountains. There was a shimmer of heat all around them and David found himself musing on the brevity of the Alaskan summer, the urgency of the need for birds and animals to get their young launched quickly before the long winter set in again.

The sun began to sink towards the western horizon before they stopped and David realised they were now approaching yet another inlet, a bit of a current at its mouth throwing up a choppier sea. In another minute they were through the waves and he could see that this little bay was so sheltered by towering grey walls of rock on the windward side that the water was quite smooth, reflecting the surrounding scenery as in a mirror. David was spellbound by the clarity of the air and the sudden silence as Ed cut the engine of the boat.

"We'll anchor here for the night," Ed said, casting a look of approbation at the stillness of the water. "We'll be quite settled here. Nothing will bother us. We can sleep aboard the boat, we won't bother to pitch tents until we're about to head inland."

The following morning was just as still. The occasional cry of a bird, but not much else, no other people or boats around. After breakfast they got their gear together for the trip: tents; fire-lighting equipment; some dried soups and meals, with coffee, sugar, and rice; the all-important bear spray; a collapsible kayak for crossing any small rivers they came across.

"We want to avoid carrying too much gear," Ed said, looking at the piles of camera equipment Gemma wanted to bring. "You going to carry all that?"

Gemma looked slightly embarrassed. "I know it looks a lot—but it's all pretty essential," she said. David volunteered to help her and his pack soon filled up with the sort of gadgets only professional photographers use. Once they had ferried themselves to shore with the help of the dinghy, Ed checked the boat again, starting the engine and reversing to bed the anchor down deeply.

Then they slipped and slid over the large boulders and pebbles on the beach and headed along the strip of grass by the side of the forest. It looked forbidding to David, mostly spruce, dark, the trees close together, and a lot of undergrowth. Ed seemed confident, clambering purposefully ahead along the shoreline, but David noticed that the bear-spray canister was attached to his belt, handy to use if necessary.

"Is that spray effective against bears?" he asked, affecting nonchalance. Ed grinned, sensing his concern.

"I've been roaming over this country a long time, taking people for camping trips, photography trips, fishing trips. Never had a bear need the bear spray. If one should take against us, the spray will soon see it off—it's very peppery indeed. It's hot like chilli."

"Well, that's reassuring, isn't it David?" said Gemma. Like Ed, she looked at home in the wilderness, scrutinising the sea and the mountains for likely photos even as she talked.

They carried on walking for a couple of hours in the bright sun. To David, still jet-lagged, it seemed a little like a dream. The mountains on their right, varying between six and twelve thousand feet according to Ed. The steady movement as they forged a path along the sea shore. The crunch of pebbles and shells underfoot; the occasional crow giving a raucous comment. Ed echoed the calls of the crows with practised ease, and laughed as they flapped heavily away.

"Intelligent birds, crows," he said. "Keep an eye out all the time. Feeding their young still."

"The sea's still dead calm," said Gemma. "We're lucky with the weather. Usually it rains in torrents—a lot."

"Yes. Don't know how long it's going to last, this sunny spell. Need to make the best of it."

David noticed that the choppiness of the preceding day had faded, and there was something hypnotic about the glassy swell rolling in to the shore and breaking on the pebbles and rocks. As he looked, a seal bobbed up, whiskery face like an old man's, and inspected them closely before disappearing again under the water. In the distance he could see a yacht steadily heading south. The arc of the horizon was clearly discernible and once again David felt his mood lift. Out in the distance Ed pointed at a rocky outcrop and suggested they stop for lunch. He had been foraging as they walked and soon had the stove alight, throwing in the green stuff he had picked, along with some of the dried soup, which, with crackers and along with some fruit and coffee was a welcome lunch.

After lunch they lay in the sun, snoozing for a bit before swinging their packs on their shoulders and continuing. Late in the afternoon they stopped for the night. The sun would be up for hours yet in the high Alaskan summer, and a stream flowing down to the sea over the sand in a little cove provided them with some fresh water. Above the tide line there was a patch of scrubby grass, starred with some strawberry leaves though no strawberries.

"Birds got the berries," Ed said. "Shame, they taste so good."

"Look, there are some blueberries on that bush over there," said Gemma, and taking a small pan she had soon picked a respectable number with David's help. They pitched the little one-man tents they had brought with them, and the stove was soon roaring once again while Ed stirred the pot balanced on it, appetising smells of wild plants and salmon emerging into the still air. There was rice boiling alongside. A sachet of teriyaki sauce completed the meal, stirred into the salmon, and they ate with the appetite given them by the exercise that, for David at least, was a little unaccustomed. He was glad he was wearing walking boots that had shaped themselves to his feet through long use, with little chance of chafing.

The days fell into a pattern. Breakfast, strike camp, hike, lunch, more hiking, set up camp again. Gemma was always alert to the scenery, and David and Ed waited patiently while she set up shots and took pictures. They planned to walk along the coast before striking inland up a narrow valley that would take them to a glacier. On the third day rain set in, and they got out their wet-weather gear and encased themselves in waterproofs. The clouds trailed veils of rain as the freshening wind pushed them in long dark-grey chains below the summits of the towering mountains. David had never been in so wild a place and he was impressed by the drama of the scenery and the complete desolation. They had not encountered any other people at all, apart from the yacht in the distance, and the deep sense of isolation struck David. He was not used to it; he wondered about the people who had lived in this place and were clearly no longer here. Occasionally they would pass a little heap of stones that seemed to speak of previous lives spent there. He noticed that the grey sky changed constantly in the wind; white clouds would appear, set in a monochrome panorama against the dark-grey sky and the deeper dark grey of the mountains. He wished he had the eye to take the photos that Gemma was constantly engaged in taking.

"Round the next bend, we'll see the river we need to walk alongside," said Ed, and as they rounded a headland they could see a wide river. Where it met the sea it ran fast, and the incoming breakers were interrupted in their smooth course to the rocky beach, turbulent and frothing in a mass of white water.

175

The sound of stones being rolled along by the river underlined the speed of the flow. Further inland the river spread out in braids across grey pebbles, and David could see that it would be relatively easy to cross. Different channels ran across the stones before joining up in the final rush to the sea. There were wading birds feeding in the shallows, small flocks that settled to feed and then rose up in a little group and flew further upstream or near the sea before feeding again on a little stretch of greyish sand. The mountains bordering the bay looked very high to David, and he felt that the walk up to the glacier might be quite challenging.

"It's quite something," he said as they paused by the rushing river, admiring the clear water and the view.

"Yeah. And we're not the only ones who think it's quite something," said Ed, pointing. Following the direction of his gaze David caught sight of a bear in the distance, who appeared to have seen them at the same time. It turned round and disappeared into the nearby wood, and Ed shook his head.

"Not sure if it's a good idea to follow the river," he said. "At this time of year, the bears will be making sure they're getting their fill of the salmon. Look, can you see them?" David could indeed see the salmon heading upstream and he marvelled that they could have made it through the turbulence at the river's confluence with the sea.

"Yes," Gemma said thoughtfully, sitting down on a boulder, easing her pack from her back. Her golden hair shone bright in a gleam of sun that was breaking through the clouds, and she looked upstream, clearly wondering if it might be too risky. "But, you know, we have a choice. We can either walk alongside the river, in the bushes and through the flat valley, or we can gain height and do a bit of a traverse at a higher level—perhaps just above the tree line."

"Mmm." Ed didn't sound convinced. "When I was thinking of the trip I was worried about the time of year and the route we might take. Either way, we have to run our way through the bears. We've seen so few up to now … but I think if we go along the river valley we can keep a sharp look out and avoid them …"

David wondered about this conversation. He wanted to defer to Ed's experience. He too sat down on a boulder. The straps of his pack were beginning to bite into his shoulders and he was glad of the rest. The sun was out, and it was delightfully warm. He admired the scenery. He could feel the concerns that had preoccupied him for so long beginning to drop away. This was more about survival in a wild landscape, his boots on the rattling grey pebbles, the cries of the sea-birds, the rush and roar of the surf in a desolate spot.

"Which do you think would be safest, Ed?" he said, turning to look at the older man.

"Well, that's just what I'm wondering about. It would be pretty spectacular up by the glacier." He pointed and David could see the river of ice lipping down over the edge of a valley high up above them in the far distance. It was clear that the rushing river was meltwater from the glacier—it would be icy.

"Yes—do you think that would be best?" David's voice was enthusiastic. He was keen to visit the glacier, continue the hike as they had planned, but he wanted to avoid the bears too. It was their country—they had avoided the little group of hikers so far, and Ed was clearly concerned to maintain their distance.

"I think on balance, they're going to be more interested in the salmon than in us," Ed said. "That's what I think when I plan trips like this, but the fact that we're keen to get up to the glacier complicates things a bit. Be easier if we were just going to walk along the river or along the coast …"

"Well perhaps we should do that then," said David, squinting against the sun. "Should be easy to get across the river."

"Yes, it's not too high yet with the rain. Though if we get a lot more rain that might make it quite difficult to cross … we've got the little kayak though," said Ed.

"But the thought of getting to the glacier, being able to get photos is quite a draw," Gemma said. "I can see what you mean about the safety angle. But surely if we're careful, say if we hike along the river valley, keep to the edge of the trees, keep a watch out for bears?" Her voice trailed away, as she tried to think through the various possibilities.

"Yeah, I've got the bear spray … if we keep a careful watch out. We could leave the kayak here, cache it, leave some spare dry food here, so we're not carrying too much, we can move fast." He turned to David. "What do you think? Are you on for it?"

David felt that he was with an expert on the business of avoiding bears and keeping safe.

"Oh, I'm on for it alright," he said. "I'd be very keen to make it up to the glacier—and we have got a chance to do that in—well, what do you think, about a few day's walking?"

"Less than that, it's not so far. If you both feel okay about it, I'm game for the hike." He squinted up at the sun, which was beginning to appear with more frequency in the grey clouds. "Why don't we make camp here for the night—it's about four—and get started in the morning? Have a bit of a rest this evening."

David was glad of a rest. His back was aching from his pack, and his legs were full of cramps; he wasn't used to the exercise.

They found a grassy area a little way back from the river and the sea where some trees gave shelter in the event of further rain. It was all dripping with the rain of the morning, raindrops trembling on the blades of grass and glistening in the sun. Ed set them to collecting wood. There was a lot of driftwood on the beach, some broken pieces of wood clearly from broken boxes with Chinese or Japanese writing on them, and some pieces of timber, which Ed chopped at with a little axe he carried with him.

"Get at the dry wood in the middle to start a fire with," he said, chipping expertly with the axe and a knife. Before long they had a reasonable pile of wood, and he had a blaze going in a sandy declivity. They pitched the tents, and Ed looked for a suitable tree on which to suspend their food once they had eaten, to keep it well away from the little camp, and from the bears.

"I think we need to cook away from the tents tonight," he said. "No cooking smells where we're sleeping, that the bears can associate with us. We can pitch the tents a bit later on, when we've eaten."

As a plan to keep away from the bears, this certainly found favour with David and he enjoyed the meal that Ed and he put together over the fire, the surf on the beach sounding a rhythmical bass note as the waves crashed in. He helped Ed string the food up on a rope over a tall branch to keep it safe and they pitched their tents a little way off. He was very tired and glad to crawl into his tent and read for a while in his sleeping bag while the other two chatted over the fire. It wasn't so far away that he couldn't hear their voices and he felt obscurely sad for a moment that Clara wasn't there, enjoying the trip with him. He wondered how she was getting on in Switzerland. Were she and Georg going to split up? That was the question. Sleep approaching rapidly, he began to dream, sinking down into an imagined future for himself and Clara. His dream was interrupted by the sound of Ed pitching more wood into the fire and through the tent wall he could see the fire flare up, the sparks soaring up into the sky. Not too much wind then, he thought sleepily to himself, otherwise the sparks would be drifting sideways. Despite the crackling from the fire he could hear snatches of talk from Gemma and Ed.

"What's the story with David, then Gemma, eh?" he heard Ed say. "Not attracted to him, are you? Thought your girlfriend was the one—at least, that was the story in the fall."

179

Gemma laughed.

"No, he's just a close friend. We went through a lot of the same stuff in London, finding places to live, working together, you know the sort of thing. As for Annie—well, we split up. I'm on my own at the moment."

"Me too," said Ed. "Not many women like the idea of their menfolk disappearing for most of the summer months, guiding, taking people on trips." "Yes, but if that's the way you need to earn your living ..." Gemma's voice trailed away and she yawned hugely. "No, David isn't with me—and he's on his own too, his relationship broke up a while back. But he's very caught up in trying to become a psychotherapist. He spends all his time thinking about that, seems to me."

"Is he going to become one, then?" asked Ed.

"No, they turned him down at the training place in London. What a waste. He'd make a good therapist ... and it's not like the States, there's more top-notch places there to go to train."

"Well, if he's serious he should move to the States." There was a silence and he could hear clinking as Gemma got her mug topped up with more whisky.

"Oh, he wouldn't do that in a million years. He's—well, what would you call it—in England they call it a one-trick pony."

"You mean he's fixated on the place in London?"

"Yes. It's difficult—a lot of his friends have trained—he's keen on this woman Clara, and she's trained."

"So why does he stick around? Why not do something different?"

"Good question. He's very good at what he does, working with children and families, and individual patients, but maybe he should—just to mix my metaphors—push the boat out, do something different."

He heard Ed laugh. "A one-trick pony who should push the boat out. Could he do that?"

Gemma laughed too. David chuckled to himself. A one-trick pony. He had been quite monomaniacal about the Radcliffe, it was true. He had focused on getting in, he had spent vast sums of money on three sessions a week of psychotherapy with a training therapist … he had felt envious of Jack, Clara, and Georg—and all the other people in his social circle who were therapists. And it was true, what Lewis Wray had said, his social life was affected by being with people who all had the same thing in common—their involvement with the Radcliffe and their identities as therapists … but actually, the life of a psychotherapist was a hard and, paradoxically, a lonely one. He thought of the long days, seeing patient after patient in the isolation of the consulting room, going on for hour after hour … Seeing patients was performing a function, trying to help them to internalise a steady presence that could contain emotional realities, helping them to manage possibly intolerable states of mind. It wasn't the same as talking to someone socially, and David realised that actually he liked the business of working in a clinical team in the child service. The collegial contact was important to him, even though it might be loaded with all the negotiations necessary between different clinical stances and different approaches to the work. And, he said to himself, in the cosy confines of his tent, if he could laugh ruefully at hearing himself described as someone who was "addicted" to the Radcliffe, perhaps there was a sense of his concern about it draining away, leaving him freer to turn his attention to other things. What was it that Bion, the famous psychoanalyst, had said? Something along the lines of how some people's states of mind got better through analysis—but other people became psychoanalysts or psychotherapists … in other words they hadn't really got better but were still struggling with their own internal states, but this time lodging them in their patients, continuing the effort to get better … Smiling still, he fell asleep.

The next morning he was woken by the sun glowing through the top of his tent, lighting it up with an orange heat. He rolled over and peered through the flap of the tent. He was facing toward the sea; it had calmed a little overnight. The waves on the shore no longer charged in to break on the shore as though with the intention of overrunning the land. Further out he could see the same sort of slight glassy swell they had enjoyed on the trip up. In the distance he caught sight of a whale's back breaking the surface, seeming as peaceful as the scene. He thought back to the conversation he had overheard the previous evening. He wondered what he would do if he couldn't train at the Radcliffe. He felt that this was a new thought, not one he had considered before.

He extracted himself from his sleeping bag, walking over to the river to splash cold—very cold—water over himself. He even considered a dip in the sea but imagined the salt sticking to his cold body and contented himself with fresh water from the river. The light was so bright that it glistened on the droplets of water he splashed around himself. He set to work building up the fire again, feeling somehow that it might be more celebratory to have coffee brewed on the fire rather than on the mundane stove they had with them. It wasn't long before the fire was blazing, spitting and crackling with the wood he piled on it.

Ed clapped him on the back. "Alright then? Good night?"

David grinned. "Even one-trick ponies can have a good sleep now and again," he joked, and enjoyed the expression of slight nervousness crossing Ed's craggy features as he realised that the conversation, possibly rather whisky-fuelled, that he and Gemma had enjoyed the previous evening, had been overheard.

"So you heard what we were saying, then," he said.

"I did, but it was only echoing what I've been thinking myself," said David easily and emolliently, not wanting to make the other man anxious. Of course it wasn't true, he hadn't been thinking along those lines at all, caught up in the all-or-nothing urge to get on the training. A bit like the salmon, he thought, rushing upstream to where they were hatched. That's what the Radcliffe represented to so many people, he thought—a primal group where belonging seemed the most important thing, self-idealising once inside the group and tending to disparage those outside. Treating applicants rather cruelly served, he thought, to underline the exclusivity of the place, the sense that people on the inside could preen themselves on their achievement in being part of such an august institution. He realised that he was standing with his mug of coffee in hand, staring at the heart of the fire, which was burning pale now in the bright sun. Ed was looking at him with some concern.

"You off with the fairies, then?" he enquired. David laughed.

"In a way," he said. He looked quizzically at Ed. How much would he understand of his overnight change of heart, his new way of thinking? "Funny how all this," he swept a hand around at the mountains, the sea, the shining braids of the river, "gives you a different perspective on your life."

Ed stirred the fire with a long twig, nodding.

"That's true enough," he said. "Reminds me of when I split up with my partner. Couldn't stick it, the thought that I was on my own again, but had to come out guiding a group—they were French photographers, more gear than you could hardly carry—and when we were out here I just felt better about it. Makes you realise how short life is, how important it is not to waste time going for things that aren't going to work." As though to underline his words, a bear crashed suddenly out of the undergrowth beside them. There was a moment of frozen shock on both sides. David felt his heart start to pound. Was the bear going to attack them? He could hardly be more than forty feet away. For a moment the bear looked at them, and David could see each separate hair on its muzzle, could see even more clearly the fearsome teeth as its mouth hung slightly open while it considered them. Ed swung into conversational mode.

"Hi there, bear," he said calmly. "Looks like you're as surprised as we are. Sorry for being in your way just now. We're going to be going soon." The bear seemed to listen intently and then without any other sign turned and crashed back into the undergrowth, broad brown back disappearing as the forest closed behind him. They could hear him crashing away, birds squawking in alarm to mark his passage. Ed grinned at David. "He was more surprised than we were, I reckon," he said. "But if you talk to them, they seem to respond. Just as well he did, my bear spray's still in my tent."

David stood, feeling his racing heart slowly quieting down. "I suppose if they hear us coming normally they move away— but perhaps he hadn't registered we were here," he said. "The breeze is off-shore—so he wouldn't have known about us. Wouldn't have picked up our scent, I suppose."

"Mmm," said Ed, considering. "Not so sure about that. Look over there. Looks like some bear or other checked us out during the night. Though maybe it was a different one." Sure enough, there were tracks in the sand near the grassy plot where they had pitched the tents. "Perhaps he could smell the food in the tree." He went over to the tree and undid the rope holding the bag of food high up in the branches and went calmly about the business of getting out a pan and flour to make some pancakes. "If you want to pick some blueberries, we'll have a good breakfast before we get going," he said, and David took a pan and went off to forage for berries. The morning was heart-stoppingly beautiful, sun burning off wisps of mist over the river where it wound into the valley. The mountains seemed very close and had hardly any cloud over them. His feet sank into the sweet-smelling undergrowth and he soon found blueberry bushes where he set himself to pick the little berries, coming back with a good haul of the succulent little globes. Ed took them from him, added water and sugar and set the pan over the flames.

184

"I'll do the pancakes with the stove," he said. "More constant heat. Don't want to burn them." Soon he had the pan sizzling and as if drawn by the sound, Gemma crawled from her tent and stood up, sweeping her tousled gold hair from her sleepy eyes and stretching."What a good sleep! I needed that after all that hiking," she said. "Did I hear you talking about bears? What was that crashing noise?"

"That was a bear," Ed said. "Surprised to find us here. Soon hightailed it away. The fire probably scared him a bit too."

"Oh my God," said Gemma. "Missed a good photo opportunity there then. As a matter of interest, did you bring a gun with you? Just in case?"

"I thought about it," admitted Ed, smiling, eyes crinkling at the corners." But you had so much camera stuff, we just couldn't carry that as well. So it's all your fault if we get eaten …"

Gemma laughed, brushing out her hair preparatory to plaiting it behind her head in a gleaming gold braid. "Well, we should be okay with the bear spray. Never been attacked yet," she said, glancing at David and clearly picking up the attentiveness in his face as he listened to this conversation. Two people he considered old timers in the business of hiking in Alaska were expressing confidence—he should be confident too, he was saying to himself.

"Well, the key thing is that the salmon are running," Ed said, flipping a pancake and giving the blueberries a stir. "Means that the bears aren't going to be short of food. I think I'd be more alert to danger if we were a hundred miles or so inland, that's where the bears don't have so much food as they do here, down on this coastal strip where they've got the berries as well as the salmon."

David felt reassured after this conversation and, as they struck camp and cached the kayak, with some of the provisions carefully suspended in a tree overhead, the sun struck him warm across the back and he felt ready for the day's hike. They shouldered their packs and Ed set up a steady stride, following the course of the river and a little path, clearly a trail followed by wildlife through the brush that ran down to the meadow by the river.

"I heard what you were saying last night about me being a one-trick pony, Gemma," David said as they got on their way. She laughed.

"Oh, God—hope you didn't take offence at that. But it's true, David, isn't it? You wouldn't think of anything else to do, besides training as a psychotherapist?"

"To tell you the truth, I'm beginning to get a bit of perspective on the whole thing."

"Perspective?" she queried, holding aside a bramble for him to pass.

"Yes. I've spent a lot of money and a lot of time pursuing a chimera, an idealised view of what it might be like to train as a psychotherapist. But it's beginning to strike me that actually the life, the work, it's difficult. Difficult enough being a psychologist, perhaps more difficult in some ways in full-time private practice. Could be a bit isolating."

"Yes. I think you're right. I do find the institutional links I have are important, that sort of thing."

Ed, listening to this conversation going on behind him turned round. "You know, David, it's hard to give up ideas about where we want to go. I tried my hand at photography like the people I take on trips, but I found however hard I tried I couldn't seem to get the hang of making photos—you know, with my photos, a mountain was just a mountain, whereas the really talented photographers can make a real beauty of a picture of a mountain, like really special. I've had to swallow that fact, that actually I'm great at what I do, organising trips and keeping people safe from bears"—he winked at David—"but I'm not so good at the photography thing. Have to leave that to other people."

Gemma intervened quickly. "No one doubts your clinical ability, David. It's just that the Radcliffe is well known for turning people down when they apply to train, just on a whim … and it's about being able to bear that in mind, the way it's really a bit arbitrary—good people get turned down all the time. It's not personal, it's simply the way the place functions. They're looking for a way to turn people down, they want to keep it exclusive. I wouldn't have applied in London to train, wanted to come back to the States, just for that reason. I was very nervous of being turned down." She looked at him with a small downturn at the corners of her mouth and David realised for the first time that she would probably have liked to stay in London, with the people she had become friendly with, in the life she had set up for herself there.

"Shame about that, Gem," he said quietly. "It would've been really good if you had stayed in the UK …"

"Yes—well … I've made a good start of getting settled in LA notwithstanding. Nothing like a heavy training to get you well embedded in a place!" She tried to make a joke of something she clearly felt strongly about. "And I hear the stance is changing a bit at the Radcliffe now. But what about you, David? What would you do, do you think, if you were going to turn your attention to other things?"

He considered this, slowly. The family precedent was for the academic life. His father had been an academic, before his suicide. An interpreter, though, thought David to himself, not an interpreter of dreams but an expert in rendering communication intelligible across language barriers. It was due to his influence that David and his sisters spoke fluent German, and David found himself remembering his father, in the lively days before depression set in, clearly enjoying his working life, turning his facility with languages into an academic speciality. Could he do something similar, become an academic? He was just about to formulate this more clearly in his mind when he realised that Ed had stopped and was raising a warning hand, urging them to keep quiet.

"What is it, Ed?" Gemma scanned the riverside meadow, which was just coming into view through a gap in the foliage.

"It's a bear with her cubs. She's catching salmon. Look—but don't make too much noise."

David edged himself to the gap in the brush, and what he saw made him smile. Two bear cubs were plunging about in one of the little tributaries to the main river, clearly emulating their mother, who was actively in the business of trying to catch one of the salmon teeming in the river. As they watched, the mother was successful and made for the bank of the little stream, where she set about tearing at the struggling silver fish with her teeth, holding it down with one of her paws. Her cubs were soon at her side, getting their share. Suddenly alert, she raised her head and seemed to be looking straight at them. David shrank back behind the bole of the tree he was standing next to, and Ed whispered to them both.

"She's seen another bear, just up the way from us." Sure enough, another bear emerged from the undergrowth, and seemed to be making for the mother and her cubs. She abandoned the fish and galloped off, cubs close at her heels. "Male bears can be a real threat to the cubs. She's wise to get the hell out of there," said Ed. "Come on. Let's get past the bear in the trees while he's busy with the fish." Without saying any more, he strode on quickly, and David had to hurry to catch up. In a few minutes they had rounded another bend and the bear was hidden from view.

A high thin haze was working its way across the sky from the south, and Ed looked up at it as it began to veil the sun. "Think we're in for a bit of weather again soon," he said. There wasn't much more conversation about David's future but as he got into the rhythm of the hiking and following the other two as they made their way along the little path winding alongside the banks of the river, he became lost in thought. It seemed that he was once again in the garden in the family home, cat sunning itself between the apple trees, the privet hedge giving off a spiced sweetness, his father digging the vegetable patch as he and his sister played in the little sandpit outside the back door. Perhaps he could reorientate himself. His choice of a clinical life, he felt, had been dictated by his concern and guilt about his father's state of mind. But he wasn't responsible for that; he didn't need to make a masochistic choice of career that involved looking after ill people arduously for many years. Could he himself become an academic? He stopped short in the path, struck by this idea, and had to hurry a moment later, pack bumping awkwardly on his back, to catch up with the others. He was familiar with the idea that looking after people for extended periods was a masochistic choice of profession, but not so familiar with the idea that actually he didn't have to do it. But what sort of academic life could he pursue? He was still struggling with this when it began to rain, drops pattering on the leaves of the trees all about them, and they stopped to get out wet-weather gear.

"Don't like the look of this," Ed said, shrugging his pack on again over his waterproofs, grimacing at the cold drops. "Could really set in."

They pitched camp that night just below the tree-line, rigging up the tents under a spruce with spreading branches to keep off the worst of the rain. The wind was getting up too, sighing and roaring in the trees, and to David it sounded like winter days in Switzerland, along with the cold sharpness of the scent of resin from the spruce trees. They huddled round the fire they had set into a rocky overhang to keep off some of the wet. Somehow the conversation ran back to David's future plans and Gemma was keen on his new idea of an academic life. "You could do a PhD," she said enthusiastically. "Research."

189

"Yes, sure, I'd love all that work!" David teased her. "It's alright to recommend for someone else that they work themselves into the ground!" She laughed too, but the idea took hold with David, and continued all through the next day as they hiked glacier-wards. They began to walk along the river again, over a high plateau. Lumps of ice from the glacier, as big as cars, shifted and groaned audibly under the pressure of the water as they drifted downstream. Not many bears up here, Ed told them. He hoped they would all be behind them, feasting on the salmon to build up strength for the winter ahead.

"Feels like winter now," said David, squinting through the rain as it pelted into his face. He was clammy in his waterproofs and glad when they pitched camp again that night in a dryish gully where the pine needles made a soft brown carpet on the ground. For once, Ed couldn't find a tree solid enough to suspend their provisions from and he looked worried.

"Don't want to have the food too near us tonight. Not enough earth on the ground over the rock to bury it. That's what we should really do, to avoid attracting any bears," he said, and then, with what David thought was mock confidence, "Should be okay."

They settled down for the night with the food some distance from them, but even so David felt unaccountably nervous. For the first time on the trip he wished he was back in his warm, dry flat, and he shivered miserably in his sleeping bag, still damp. He didn't think that he would sleep but he was just drifting into the pre-sleep relaxation of muddled thoughts when he thought he heard a stick snap sharply and he startled fully awake again. He wondered if it could be a stick snapping in the fire—Ed had fed the fire before going to his tent and it was burning brightly—but it seemed unlikely. He listened carefully, straining to catch any further noise. There was silence; all was still. For the second time he began to drift towards sleep only to hear a snuffling noise. This must surely be a bear, he thought, after their provisions—or after him and the others. He called to Ed, who looked worried as he emerged from his tent, light still there in the summer night sky. David scrambled from his sleeping bag and looked out of the flap of his tent, cold droplets of rain splashing on his face unheeded.

"What can you see, Ed?" he hissed quietly. Ed held up a warning hand, and pointed. To David's alarm he could see a bear on the other side of the gully, catching sight of them and clearly surprised, but still showing an alert interest in the pack of food they had stowed under a heap of stones before going to bed. The bear seemed huge, and David could distinctly see the rain gleaming on its pelt. Its claws and teeth were very visible too and as he saw them David felt momentarily dizzy with fright. Just breathe, he said to himself, and the frozen scenario suddenly splintered as Ed tripped momentarily and almost fell. Ed swore to himself softly and David reached back into his tent purposefully for his own pepper spray.

"That's good, David," said Ed. "We need to frighten this bear away. It's too dangerous for him to link us with the food—might think we'd make good eating. Just grab the other side of my tent, let's rip it out of the ground and flap it at him, and shout out loud at the same time." Suiting his action to his words, he suddenly ripped the tent from its supporting ropes and pegs and flung it up in the air. "Grab the other side, David!" he shouted, and the two of them flapped the tent and shouted at the bear, while Gemma crawled from her tent, roused by the noise. The bear turned tail and fled, and David let out a gasp of relief. But the relief was short-lived; the bear stopped and turned, looking at them, it seemed to David, in a considering way.

"It doesn't seem to be scared, Ed," he said, and Ed muttered under his breath, something along the lines that this sometimes happened with a persistent and hungry bear.

"We'll have to try something a little more heavy-weight," Ed said, looking round thoughtfully. There was a dreadful pause while the bear looked at them, and Ed stood motionless, clearly racking his brains for something that would protect them from the unwanted interest of this large creature. It sank on to all fours and ambled back towards the food, taking no notice of them.

"It won't be long before he discovers there's nothing much there for him," Ed said. "I think the best plan is to frighten him off with some firebrands. Let's get the fire going again," and he reached for some dry wood he had chipped away at earlier, and got it roaring on the fire.

"Help me here David," Ed muttered, and the two of them set to work to get the fire burning. In the glow of the fire and the dim light under the trees, David could see Gemma looking wordlessly at them and at the bear who was pawing at the food, snuffling and grunting. The bear looked very ferocious to David, and he felt a real determination scare it away.

"Okay, what we need to do, David, is to get out some flaming pieces of wood and run towards the bear with them, throw them. You too, Gemma. We really need to scare this one off. Here, you take this chunk of wood, Gemma, get it burning brightly at one end." He stirred up the fire vigorously, and embers and sparks flew upwards. The bear looked towards them, apparently nervous now. David was glad that Ed seemed so resourceful. He thought that between the three of them there was a chance of making the bear flee.

"Ok, have each of you got a burning bit of wood? Then let's run at him on the count of three." He counted, shouting as he reached three and charged at the bear waving a large firebrand. David and Gemma followed him, David almost losing his footing in the gully on the rough stones. Ed threw the firebrand at the bear, which growled, standing on its hind legs, and David realised that Ed was also firing off his pepper spray at it. The combination of firebrands and fiery pepper spray was too much for the bear, which turned and crashed away through the trees.

"Thank God for that," said Gemma, panting with the exertion of the sudden run across the gully. "I don't think I'm going to go back to sleep after that."

"No, I think we need to keep the fire banked up all night and get the hell out in the morning," said Ed.

The fire was kept up all night and they took it in turns to doze and keep it banked up. As they got up to get going David could see, in the grey light, that Gemma looked strained and pale, and he imagined he looked the same.

"Let's move on quickly," said Ed, and they packed up the tents and their packs, moving off without stopping to have breakfast. It was drizzling, cloud down over the tops of the mountains and they seemed in a little world of their own. They made good time up to the glacier and there were no further sightings of the bear. The glacier was a magnificent sight, even in the mist, its foot in a lake that was black and still, apart from when large chunks of ice fell into it from the glacier with a thunderous noise.

They camped for the night nearby and in the morning David woke to bright sunshine striking his tent and the sound of the camp fire crackling as Ed prepared morning coffee for them. They hiked round the side of the lake and got close to the glacier, David marvelling at the intense blue of the ice interspersed with grainy grey-and-black patches where it had scraped against valley walls. This was the highlight of the trip and later, thinking back, David was glad that they had persevered in their attempt to get to the glacier and hadn't allowed the bear to frighten them back down the mountain. They had no further trouble with bears on the return journey, and even the sea trip back to the little town was calm and trouble-free.

# EIGHTEEN

B ack in the UK and at work, David felt that it had been something of a dream. After a week of seeing his patients and the families in the child and adolescent service, he felt that he had never been away, getting over the customary return-to-work difficulty far more speedily than usual. He was impatient to see Clara again, but she seemed still to be away, her phone unanswered. His flat seemed small and cluttered when he looked around it after his trip, and he spent some time clearing it and doing some decorating, painting the hall a pale shade of grey, as suggested by Marie. Over the dinner he had with her and Jack, they listened to his traveller's tales, enthralled. They were clearly feeling somewhat tied down by the demands of parenthood. He was glad to see them again, and glad to see his colleagues at work and his patients. He felt that the trip away had been a transformative one; he could see the value of the work he was doing with the families. He was less inclined to regard the work as of lesser status than private work as a psychotherapist, and therefore as less worthwhile. Looking at himself in the mirror one morning in September he saw an older, more sober face looking back at him, definitely with some grey hairs now.

Thea, the child psychiatrist, put her head round his door not long after he had got back.

"Mind if I come in? Are you busy?" she asked, and when he indicated that she could come in, sitting back from his computer at his desk, she came and placed her large bulk in one of his four chairs, moving surprisingly lightly for such a large person. David joined her, sitting down in one of the other chairs, facing her.

"Did you have a good summer, Thea?" he said. "Haven't got round to asking you." She gave him a description of her holiday in France, enlivened by visits to Cathar castles—she was a keen historian. David had got used to this interest of hers, which he shared, and he liked her descriptions of the places she had visited and the history. He was pleased that she had come to his room to involve him in conversation. There was a pause. Through the wall David could hear a raised voice as a parent berated a child in the middle of a session, and the calm tones of Selena breaking in to comment in a containing way.

"Lively times," he said to Thea, as much to break the silence as to comment on the noise from the consulting room next door.

"Yes, that was what I was going to speak to you about, David," she said. "I wanted to talk to you about two things." David had a slightly nervous sense that she was about to ask him to do something that he didn't want to do, in addition to his normal work load.

"I wondered whether you could see your way to preparing a paper to give at the conference coming up in the spring, about your work here in the service? The other thing I wanted to ask you was whether you thought it might be time to run another adolescent group. We have a number of adolescents who need therapy, but for whom there is a long wait to be seen by one of the child psychotherapists. What do you think?" She glanced at David, and seeing his face expressing doubt, his mouth down-turned, wondering whether he could say that actually he had more than enough work on his plate, she laughed but said no more. Her skirt glowed in the sunshine from the window, gold flecks sparkling in the material, and David thought irrelevantly and not for the first time how well she dressed, and that he liked the clothes she wore in carefully put-together outfits. He ran a hand through his hair, now flecked with grey, and raised his eyebrows heavenwards.

"Do you remember the last group I ran with Selena, Thea?" he asked her.

"I do, David, and it was such a success! Even a *succès fou*, I would say," she beamed, and then began something of a statement about the value of it, and the value of this work to the service, so much so that David stopped listening and sank into a daydream as he thought back to the last meeting of the group.

He was as sure of the value of the group to the participants as Thea was, but, thinking about it, he wondered if in fact he had underplayed the achievements of the group. All the participants had gone on to do well at school, and he imagined that they were now launched from their school careers into whatever the future had held for them. He remembered with painful clarity the last session, with each of the young people expressing their upset at the ending in their own ways. Victor, the Polish boy who had started the group nervously, had become much more self-assured, but had regressed in the last few sessions of the year to a lot of silence and foot-tapping. In the last session he had asked, with a clearly distressing sense of the difficulty of saying anything at all in the hearing of his peers, whether he could continue to be seen. The group had become very important to him, and David had been forced to comment that Victor wasn't able to imagine that, actually, he would manage without it, that other interests would come to the fore in his mind once the group stopped and he had processed the difficult feelings of mourning that went with the loss of it. In fact, David had later heard from Victor's school, when he went in to discuss another student causing concern, that Victor was much more settled and personable. He was doing well academically and in his relationships with the other students.

He mused on as Thea continued to talk. Tina, the bright girl, had been a helpful and intelligent presence right up until the end of the group and, predictably, was doing well. Sevda, the Turkish girl, had come to value the group considerably and, perhaps because the ending was unbearable, had missed the last session and had refused any further appointments. She was doing marginally better at school, seeming a little happier, and had avoided being sent back to Turkey by her father, who had threatened to do so unless she attended to her school work and was more obedient at home. Vi, the lively girl, was more settled. All in all, he mused, it was not unimpressive as a first attempt on his part at running a group for adolescents along with Selena, the child psychotherapist. He emerged from his consideration of the group to find that Thea had stopped talking and was looking at him in silence.

"Sorry, Thea, I missed the last bit that you said?" She drummed her fingers irritably on the wooden arm of her chair.

"I had a feeling you were thinking about something else," she said. "I was just asking you whether you felt able to run another group, and give a talk at the conference. The specialist work that you do with parents, alongside the work of the child psychotherapists, is very highly valued in the team. I know there's an increasing strain, with the waiting list being so long, and the pressure being to see families for a four-session bit of work, what they call an episode of care." She frowned and said heavily, "But you and I both know that if difficulties aren't dealt with in a proper and substantial way, families are simply back in another couple of months with the same problem or something slightly different. It used to be called the revolving door, didn't it? It's really a waste of resources as well as distressing and damaging for the families not to be seen in an appropriate way in the first place, with some sense being made of their difficulties ... we are a specialist service, are we not?" He nodded. He agreed with her; he could not abide the new pressure from management to get through the waiting list quickly by offering families less than what was adequate to deal with their difficulties. "You wouldn't treat a brain tumour with an aspirin, would you?" she added. Thea wasn't usually so forthright, tending to be diplomatic and, in public at least, stressing the value of short-term work aimed at changing behaviour without any thought for the underlying dynamics of the family.

"The service needs adequate resourcing," he said. "No point in pretending that the work is going to be done when everyone knows it's chronically underfunded."

"Well, it's what the taxpayer will bear with," she sighed. She flicked an imaginary speck of dust from her skirt. "Well, David, would you like to think about the paper? And the group for adolescents?"

"I'll do the paper," he said with a firmness of purpose that surprised him. Had he been taken in by the way that she stressed the value of the work he did? He decided that it was of value to put the work out more firmly into the public domain: the way that parents needed support and to be understood, when they brought their children to the child and adolescent service; the necessity of making sense of the family's difficulties in the light of the internal worlds of both children and parents. He thought it was a valuable enterprise and he said so. And added that he didn't have the time at the moment to run another adolescent group. Perhaps after the conference.

"Well, it was asking a lot, to ask you to tackle a big chunk of work like that as well as write a presentation for the conference. Perhaps I can ask Selena to involve one of the child psychotherapists to join her," Thea said. He was discomforted by this, liking the working relationship that he had with Selena. He felt that he might be quite unsettled by such a vital piece of work going to someone else. Thea noticed his hesitation, and there was a slight hint of schadenfreude in her expression as she smiled and said, with a firm reasonableness, that there was no hurry and that she would come back to him in a few months' time. "Incidentally, I wondered what had happened with your last application to the Radcliffe?" she asked and looked cast down when David said that the application hadn't been successful. He was certain that these things were gossiped about, and he was surprised that she didn't already know. She was a psychotherapist, involved there, although the bulk of her work was done in the NHS.

"That must have been a disappointment for you," she said. "I'm surprised they turned you down ..." then added blandly that perhaps there had been some anxiety about him, and he was immediately infuriated. How much would it cost her to support a colleague whose valuable work she had been praising two minutes previously? But, he supposed in a philosophical moment, perhaps, like all the people who orbited the Radcliffe, the most important thing for her was her membership of the organisation; she probably didn't feel that a protest from her would make much difference. He was aware that she did not rely on the Radcliffe for her work, so that she might have been expected to have a little more independence of mind, but it was clear where her first loyalty lay.

Later, discussing the conversation with his psychotherapist, he found himself up against the usual feelings. As he spoke about Thea's response to the news that he had not been accepted he mused aloud on her loyalty to the Radcliffe, and his irritation with that, to have Darwin comment drily that he imagined that his feelings about Thea were in some way relevant to his feelings about the therapy; wasn't it the case that Alexander himself was a person who orbited the Radcliffe?

"Yes, but you're different. I can see that you have some reservations about the way people are treated at the Radcliffe, whereas Thea was quite happy to dismiss my experience as being to do with a fault in me, some anxiety about me, rather than seeing the organisation as being at fault for not taking on someone who had, in her view, quite a lot to offer."

He heard Darwin sigh slightly behind him and realised that they were on familiar territory. Not for the first time he mentally set aside his experience with the Radcliffe as being of the sort that brought back to life his early infantile experience of being in the incubator for long weeks, excluded from human warmth, and unendurable because of that. Of course, he said to himself, he was vulnerable because of his early experience; he quoted to himself the line about the child being father to the man. He would necessarily be more sensitive to the way the Radcliffe treated people, but in fact he could think it through; his own susceptibility, but also his capacity to develop a different mind-set. This was a view based on a clarity of vision, both about what he might bring to the experience, but also the failings of the organisation. As he remarked to Darwin, did he now want to continue to lament his fate as one of the excluded, or did he want to develop a different capacity in himself? As he talked about his wish to move forward, perhaps academically, he heard Darwin shift in his chair behind him as the interest and excitement with which he talked began to make an impact on him.

"This is really quite a change," Darwin said. "You seem to have moved on in your thinking while you were away." David laughed.

"Nothing like a life-threatening encounter with a bear to make you realise that life is short and it's important not to waste time!" he said. Actually he could hear for himself the change in his voice as he talked with enthusiasm about the possible courses of action open to him.

"I'm wondering in fact whether the child and adolescent service would be interested in sponsoring me in an academic way ... although given the economic situation I can't imagine that they would support me financially, but they might be willing to give me some time to study, to move forward … I remember the manager of the service saying that management like to feel that they're developing their personnel."

"Do you think that wanting to move on in the academic sphere has to do with wanting to stay linked in with your father? He was an academic, wasn't he?" Darwin's comment shook David momentarily. He remembered the pride he felt in his father's status as an academic, the books and papers he had published.

As a small boy he had liked to be in his father's study while he worked, reading books, writing. The sound of the clock ticking on the mantelpiece, the slight noise as his father turned the page in the book he was studying. David reflected on the fact that his father was a bit like Charles Darwin, who was an involved father. He knew that when Darwin's children were ill, they would be tucked up on the sofa in his study whilst he worked at his desk. He remembered being uncharacteristically quiet in his father's study, busying himself with reading or writing too, or putting together intricate models. Normally he was an active boy, liking to be out in the garden, or playing with the other neighbourhood boys out in the street with his bike, but there was something special about the time he spent quietly in his father's room. He liked the atmosphere in the room with its book-lined walls, its neatly arranged files and papers, the slightly less neat arrangement of plants on the window sill. The Persian carpet covering the wooden floor felt smooth to his touch as he sprawled on the floor, and he always felt pleased when his father addressed a quiet word or two to him. Sometimes one of his sisters would try to inveigle him out to the garden, but often he would be left in peace.

He was sufficiently interested in the possibility of a change of direction that he arranged a meeting with his manager to discuss the possibility of time off to pursue academic work. Before that could happen, though, he had a phone call from Clara. He was delighted that she was back; even more delighted to hear her story of the events of her holiday. She had come home early, after discovering that Georg had invited his parents to share their holiday house in the Swiss mountains without asking her. He was being typically high-handed, she complained bitterly to David as they met over coffee at the weekend.

"I'm not surprised you didn't like that," David said soothingly. The light from the large Georgian windows of the café fell full on her, and the sun lit up her hair in a most fetching way, and once again he admired the green colour of her eyes as she glanced at him. He found, when he glanced again, that to his consternation there were tears in her eyes. They threatened to brim over. He reached over the table and patted her hand where it lay next to her coffee cup. In his mind, the lively noise around them in the café receded into the background. It was a particularly noisy place with wooden floors and lots of children out with their parents. The busy atmosphere and the smell of coffee usually suited him well, but today it was too loud and lively for him.

"What's wrong? Is it Georg?" he asked her. She responded gratefully to his sympathetic tone, and clutched his hand for a moment, convulsively. She took out a tissue from her stylish black leather bag and dabbed at her eyes with it.

"It's silly to be so upset," she said, trying to smile through her tears. "I saw it coming. I knew it was going to happen sometime."

"What was going to happen?" He didn't need really to ask the question. He knew the answer.

"He's found someone else. There's a *friend*"—she hissed the word in a venomous way—"he's been seeing on his trips. He said he had to do teaching, and I believed him—in fact he was doing teaching, because he kept telling me about the details of the seminars he was running, little stories about the students and so on—but while he was doing that, he was also seeing this friend. He told me about it just before I came back to London. In fact I came back to London because of that, not because he had invited his parents along for the holiday without asking me … it was awful. So embarrassing—it was so public because I had to explain to his parents why I wasn't going to be staying for the holiday." Irrelevantly, she said, "And it was a lovely house, too … a setting high up in the mountains, near a lake. It could have been such a wonderful holiday." She stifled a sob, and sipped her coffee, then taking out a spoon stirred it viciously and fast, clanking the spoon against the side of the cup. The couple sitting at the next table looked at her curiously. A little boy laughed at the sight of another little boy falling over on a scooter outside the window, and was shushed rapidly by his mother.

"How very difficult for you. It must have been a real problem to extricate yourself from that situation with his parents." He looked at her and she noticed the concern in his voice and smiled a small smile of gratitude.

"That bit of it wasn't too bad. He drove me to the airport and I got a flight back. I moved out of the house as soon as I got back, really. I'm staying with Miranda—you remember her?" He did, vaguely; a tall woman with sculptured black hair and very red lipstick. "She's been wonderful—thankfully she has a spare room, so that I can stay there for a bit."

"But what about your cat? And it's your house, isn't it?" David could not imagine the practicalities of the situation. Her eyes filled with tears again. "Yes, it's very difficult. That's why I didn't get in touch with you. I couldn't face anyone really. I didn't want to stay in the house on my own waiting for Georg to come back and then for him to leave. He's doing the kind thing. He's renting a flat himself so that I can move back into my house … he's looking after Pamina for me." Her face crumpled, only to dissolve into slightly hysterical giggles when he looked incredulous and asked who Pamina was.

"The cat of course!" she laughed.

"But what a name for a cat!" He was relieved to see her regain some capacity to laugh and he persevered with the subject. "How did she come by a name like that?"

"Oh—I saw the Ingmar Bergman film of *The Magic Flute*!" she said as though this was an explanation.

"And?" he said, grinning at her. She laughed too and explained: that Pamina was the name of the heroine, the one who had to deal with life's trials and tribulations; her admiration for Bergman's cinematography; the wonderful scene where Pamina was dissuaded from suicide by the intervention of the three boys, singing with bright treble voices. Her face clouded again and she clearly could not be distracted long from her sense of betrayal and wounded pride.

"I know this is going to sound rather spineless—I mean, you live on your own, don't you?" Clara said. He nodded. Not through choice, he said to himself, but she was off again on the difficulty of her situation. "You see, I've never lived on my own." She went on to describe her acquisition of the house through an inheritance from her grandmother. How lovely it had been to fill it with student friends when she had been studying at university. She had always had someone to live in it with her until Georg moved in and they were a couple in the house ... to do credit, she said, he had taken an interest in the house, and the garden. The grey-green painted front door was his effort. David was encouraging.

"When are you going to move back in, then?" he asked.

"When Georg finds a flat. He's looking at the moment, but he's so busy, with his work and so on ... the awful thing is that I am going to keep bumping into him at the Radcliffe. I just don't want to see him at the moment. I can't stand the sight of him."

"Well, I can understand that ... he's hurt you ... it's one thing to end a relationship and then find someone else, but to see someone whilst he's living with you ..." He nearly said that Georg was like a sailor with a girl in every port, and was then distracted by the idea that of course Switzerland had no ports, being landlocked ... he was aware that Clara was drawing patterns on the table in a spilled drop of cappuccino and added lightly, "If that was a Rorschach test, I predict it would speak volumes about your state of mind." Clara smiled absently.

"Yes. You know, I had this feeling that the relationship wasn't going anywhere, somehow. I just had this sixth sense. But why can't he move away? Why does he have to continue to be here? The psychotherapy community is such a small one— I'm going to be encountering him all the time ..."

"It's going to be very difficult to bear with that, I know," he said. "At least when Rachel and I split up, she was working somewhere else and I was going to be moving in different arenas"—he smiled at this overweening description of his working life—"in different circles, you know what I mean." She flashed a quick smile at him and nodded.

"I got the impression that actually you weren't too bothered when you split up," she said slowly, not looking at him, and he was glad of that, as he felt himself blushing. Had she guessed that he was really interested in her; that she was the person who had been occupying his mind?

"There wasn't exactly a marriage of true minds," he said, slightly abruptly to hide his confusion. "You know ... she worked in the bank. She loves music, and so do I, but just sharing one interest isn't enough really. I still encounter her at the choir, and that's alright ... she tells me that she's with someone else now—he works in the city too, nearby, and I'd guess that she's happier with that, than with someone who earns a pittance in the public sector."

"Personality and wonderful attractiveness notwithstanding, then?" she emerged from her *douleur* for a moment, long enough to tease him, green eyes darting to meet his while a smile hovered around her mouth in a way that he found enchanting.

205

"You know, you are going to cope," he said seriously. "You'll have to take it day by day. But you've got your work … your friends … and you've got me, too." He risked the last addition, carefully avoiding looking at her in case she realised that he was sweet on her, and in case he saw in her eyes an indifference towards him that he feared to see. He chided himself with his sensitivity and his nervousness; at the moment, she was in shock, mourning a relationship that had run its course. He returned hastily to practical matters. "Your parents, they live in Kent, don't they? Not far away."

"Yes, my father was a doctor there, so of course he and my mother have stayed there, lots of friends and so on. In fact I'm going to see them next weekend. My sister and her husband and kids will be there too, so it will be busy."

"Is she older or younger than you? I can't remember, you *have* told me." He sipped the last of his coffee.

"She's three years older than me. She's a doctor too, but working part-time while the kids are small. John's an English teacher—works locally, as a matter of fact."

"Oh yes, I remember now. They live nearby, don't they? Not far from you?" She nodded.

"It's been great having them so close. And it's meant that I can be around with the kids, help out, that sort of thing."

"What age are the children?"

"Kenny is ten—he's lovely, very quiet and always has his nose in a book, like his dad. Margarita is eight, wants to go into the theatre, belongs to a kid's drama group, and actually she is a bit of a drama queen! She has to be the centre of attention but that's fine, that suits Kenny actually, gives him the space. He's already doing little bits of writing, had a piece in the local paper."

"Really?" said David, impressed. "What about?"

"Oh, it was about the way the council are letting the local café in the park go to rack and ruin. He got a picture of it in the paper with his little piece, and it was quite something. They made a big fuss of him about it at school."

David was relieved that Clara seemed to retrieve some sense of cheerfulness as they talked over coffee. Over the weekend he had the comfortable sense that their relationship might be as much in the forefront of her mind as it was in his.

## NINETEEN

The autumn passed pleasantly enough. Clara moved back into her house, and continued to lament her relationship with Georg. Towards Christmas, David was startled one morning to get a letter from the Radcliffe. It seemed to indicate that the change of stance there, hinted at by Jack, had become a reality. The letter invited him to meet with a member of the group tasked with assessing new applicants for training. It let him know that this was on the basis that they were revisiting all the applicants who had been rejected in the previous ten years. David could hardly believe his eyes as he read it. It was such a contrast to the letters he had received previously, which had been curt and dismissive. This one, welcoming in tone, spoke of a major change in attitude to applicants.

He could hardly wait to discuss the content of the letter with Jack, and as it was a Saturday morning he had arranged to go for a run with him. He had the letter with him when they met. "What on earth's going on there?" he asked Jack. They had sat down in his car before starting on their run in order to give the letter their full attention, and to get away from the cold. It was a sunny day, but the leaves were off the trees now and the mid-November sunshine was thin. The smell of decaying leaves was everywhere, and the bare branches of the trees dripped. Where the odd leaf hung on to a tree there was a flash of amber light. David was glad of his fleece and the warmth of the car.

"You know it's what I was telling you about," Jack said. "There's a change of climate at the Radcliffe. There are too few people coming forward to train. There aren't enough people to deal with the work. They can't maintain the stance nowadays that they developed in the seventies, with lots of trainees and a lot of interest generally in psychoanalytic thinking. People find it difficult to afford three sessions a week for psychotherapy. The number of people able to afford the money—and time—for that has dwindled. And I do think that many people feel that intending trainees haven't been properly treated."

"You can certainly say that," said David with some feeling. "But isn't there a hard core, a group of people who want things to stay as they are? I always thought that if there were to be any change there, it would take a lot of time."

"That's right. There is actually a group of people who have full private practices, who are senior and who are often involved in the training, who want to keep things as they are. You know the sort of thing—I'm doing alright, so I'm not bothered about change. They want to keep the Radcliffe small, just as it's always been. But now even they realise that it's too small."

David was silent for a moment. The trees dripped on to the roof of the car. He remembered a colleague of his, a very bright and able young woman, a psychologist, who had approached the Radcliffe for training … and had been told to go away and have years of psychotherapy first. She had gone away and trained as a family therapist with the Limes clinic instead. And he could imagine that there were a lot of other people who had been put off training as psychotherapists in exactly the same high-handed way. He thought with warmth of his colleague, bright and able woman that she was, and lamented for a moment what had happened. She would have been such an asset to the Radcliffe, and of great value to her patients now as a psychotherapist.

"Do you think that the Radcliffe's change of heart's going to last?" he asked. It was helpful that Jack was heavily involved at the place, and seemed to know what was going on there.

"Well, you know, I do think so. In the bad old days of treating applicants appallingly, and being the sort of place that withdrew into exclusivity and a defensive and barricaded stance that led to a ridiculous grandiosity and self-idealisation, it might have been a short-lived change. But now things have moved on so much. The people in charge are thoughtful about the organisational issues. They're thoughtful about the Radcliffe's place in the psychotherapy world. They realise that being more inclusive as an organisation is the right way forward. Not only because it's the right thing to do, but because they have a new awareness that they need to safeguard their reputation as an organisation committed to its trainees as well as to the furtherance of psychoanalytic thinking."

"They're obviously realising that they've been rather misguided!" David laughed. He was familiar with the issue: the decline in the number of trainees, perhaps because of the difficulty of earning a precarious living in the field working privately, but nevertheless a steady demand for psychotherapy from people who were struggling.

David was impressed despite himself. He had been bitter about his treatment at the hands of his interviewers, and had been inclined to look elsewhere for career development. But the evidence that he held in his hands, the letter, was of a profound change in the organisational atmosphere of the place. But perhaps he should consider it very carefully. "Come on, Jack," he said, opening the car door. "Let's get going. Be lunchtime soon, and that little one of yours won't wait for his lunch, even if his Dad is out in the fresh air getting fit."

After their run David went back to Jack and Marie's for lunch. He always enjoyed getting together with the two of them and their little boy, and later on in the day he returned to his own flat with a pleasant sense of having had a good day with close friends. He was due to go out with other friends that evening, and he decided to read for a while before getting ready. He could not concentrate. The letter was putting paid to his peace of mind. He thought with some irritation to himself that this was the way of it, that any contact with the Radcliffe provoked some feelings, whether of a bitter sense of exclusion or a grudging admiration. Today the admiration was less grudging than usual. He was able to be impressed by an organisation that could reflect on its own process and reorientate itself. A different stance towards the external world was necessary, given the changes in the world around them. There were many more psychotherapy organisations now, and people could go and train at any number of them. Perhaps there was competition for trainees, and perhaps the Radcliffe was revisiting its previous applicants in order to acquire trainees before other organisations did, and to bolster its numbers. It seemed to be a situation, he reflected to himself, where a little competition was a good thing. It had prompted the Radcliffe to revise its stance to the external world and to future trainees. It was a bit like the reconciliation process that always needed to happen, whether in Northern Ireland or in South Africa. A capacity to engage in dialogue, even with so-called terrorists, to address transgressions …

Overall, he decided, wandering restlessly around his flat, he was pleased to be invited to be reconsidered. But should he accept the offer? What about his academic ambitions? He wondered, however, if the academic life might be rather arid. He liked the personal contact of working with patients and families, as well as colleagues. He could see that getting into the academic life might be very satisfying, but he couldn't

211

quite see in what area. He could take forward the psychology, he supposed. It would all need some thinking about, and he had to admit to himself that his state of mind was one of suppressed excitement, with an uncertainty about how to proceed. He would have liked to talk to Clara about it, but she was busy visiting her parents for the weekend. Her mother had recently had a fall, and was in hospital, and there was a need for her to be on hand at the weekend when she could get away from work.

He was glad to get back to his therapy on the Monday, and to review the situation with Darwin. The brightness of the weekend had given way to dull, misty weather, with the acrid smell of fireworks from bonfire night the previous week still in the air. He could tell that Darwin was not surprised to hear of his letter, and had a sixth sense that he might well have been one of the modernisers at the Radcliffe, wanting the place to move out of its moribund state. He thought that Darwin was encouraging. Rules had changed, and he could now be a training therapist for David, to take him through the training as required, should he decide to approach the Radcliffe again, and should he be accepted. David picked up on a note of caution, and wondered how easy he would find it to deal with, should he be turned down yet again. But would they do that, when some people there had actually decided to contact him to invite him to a meeting? He supposed it was within the realms of possibility, and it would be mortifying … but more to the point, he would find it difficult to forgive himself if he turned down this opportunity.

It wasn't until after Christmas that it was possible to arrange to meet with a member of the Radcliffe. It had snowed during the night, and David was relieved that the distance he had to travel to the meeting wasn't great and he could manage on foot. The sound of the traffic was dimmed, the branches of the trees were heavy with snow, and, as he walked, it dropped softly on to the pavement, the sound clearly audible in the silence. The fresh snow gave out a sound of its own as he compacted it underfoot in walking along. He tried to characterise it in his mind; it wasn't a squeaking noise exactly, nor a crunching noise. It wasn't freezing hard enough for that. More a soft creaking noise. He turned into the street where the psychotherapist he was to see lived. He had been instructed to go down the steps to the basement, and he could see from footsteps in the snow that he wasn't one of the first to be there. Like many therapists, Freya Woburn was clearly someone who started work early so that she could see patients before they needed to get to work. He stamped the snow from his feet and rang the bell, and was welcomed by someone who seemed to be prepared to treat him in a friendly and ordinary way. No sign of the coolness and distance he had become used to in interviews, where each interview was treated as a clinical encounter and he was dealt with in an impersonal way.

She invited him to sit down pleasantly. She was a thin woman, elderly, with warm but elegant clothes, gold jewellery, her grey hair cut stylishly. The room was like so many consulting rooms—wooden polished floorboards with a bright rug on the floor, books lining one wall, a window out to the front with antique lace curtains concealing the room from passers-by on the street above. To his surprise he found that in the fireplace there was a wood-burning stove, which was actually alight, and the fire crackled as it consumed the wood that had clearly just been loaded into it. On the mantelpiece above stood a mirror with gilded edges and in front of the mirror were two or three orchids in bowls, making a pleasing spring-like contrast to the snowy winter weather outside the window. He liked the room, and he was disposed to like Freya Woburn too. She sat back in her chair and regarded him with a smile.

"You had a letter from the Radcliffe, of course," she said.

"Yes, I was invited to meet with someone to review the decisions made in relation to my previous applications," he said, nervous now that the moment of meeting had arrived. What was she going to suggest?

"There's been something of a change at the Radcliffe," she said. "We're revisiting the applications of people who were turned down in the last ten years. There has been a general recognition that the Radcliffe has been rather too exclusive in its dealings with possible trainees … unnecessarily so. It was thought that many of the people who were turned down would welcome the chance to be reconsidered, if offered the opportunity … and I gather, from the fact that you accepted the offer of a meeting with me, that you might be one of those people?" She looked at David. David was inclined to be combative, and to suggest that really an apology might be in order, to address the feelings he had about the way that he had been treated. But then he suddenly remembered his father telling him that never apologising or explaining could be one way forward for organisations to deal with difficulties. He cleared his throat.

"I'm glad that there has been a change of heart. I must confess to having been surprised that an organisation that attends to the internal world could be so exclusive. Everyone knows that reasonable people have been turned down for no very good reason." She smiled, to his surprise, at his clear criticism. She remarked that she had heard the Radcliffe described as a place that tried to find reasons for not accepting people to train, rather than being delighted that people were applying and, in fact, doing their best to make it possible for them to become psychoanalytic psychotherapists. She referred to the fact that she had worked for a long time at the Limes clinic, and had found that their stance was much more inclusive. It had led, for example, to psychotherapy trainees being offered publically funded posts to train, so that there wasn't an insistence on private practice being the only way of working … she paused and David found himself nodding. He had noticed the same thing. The inclusiveness of the Limes clinic had always found favour with him.

"I had noticed the same thing about the Limes clinic," he said. "Of course, it's turning into a shadow of its former self because of all the cuts the Tories are making."

"I agree." She shook her head sadly and went on. "In my day it really was a centre of excellence, with people coming from all over the world to train there. As I understand it, there's constant pressure now to offer short-term work to people despite the complexity of the patients' presentation. Episodes of care. And the funding's being withdrawn constantly too, so that all the contracts from the local authorities aren't coming to the Limes. People are being offered local services instead, often given treatment by practitioners who can offer brief behaviourally-focused counselling-type interventions but who are at sea when called on to make some sense of the complex difficulties they're being presented with."

David responded eagerly. "Yes, it's the same thing happening in child and adolescent services. The other day I worked with a young colleague in seeing a family and at the end of the meeting I asked her what her qualifications were, as she was expressing interest in working with the parents. It turned out that she was a psychology graduate with no clinical training or qualifications. None. It's really a question of fools rushing in where angels fear to tread. No work being offered to people where meaning can be thought about, teased out … no containment in the work. It's going to be episodes of care, with families being positively damaged by being offered, for example, behavioural work when there might be complex issues of, well, for example, intergenerational transmission of trauma …"

He was pleased to see that Freya Woburn was nodding, clearly in sympathy with what he was saying. There was a silence for a minute, the fire crackling behind the glass door of the little stove, and David noticed with pleasure the faint trace of wood smoke in the air.

"There is a lot to recommend private practice, I find," she said. "I did find the difficulty in acknowledging the fact that patients were being given short shrift was painful. One had to pretend that short-term work might well be the treatment of choice, when everyone—clinicians, I'm talking about, not managers—knew that long-term treatment was required. At least there is research that demonstrates the value of long-term work, where there are cases that are complex. But we mustn't be side-tracked, and I want to acknowledge to you what people at the Radcliffe feel, that your application was blocked, when really there was no good reason for that having happened."

David was surprised. He could not have foreseen the generosity of this open acknowledgment.

"Yes, I did feel blocked," he said simply. "The difficulty for me was that the repeated applications I was invited to make over a number of years resulted in my putting off other courses which I could have pursued, because I felt convinced in my own mind that I was someone who had a lot to contribute, both to the Radcliffe, and to patients … and that I would be accepted at some point. Of course, that view was proven to be wrong … I was turned down finally after many years of paying for three-times-a week therapy with a training therapist. At vast expense I may say … testing my financial resources. And then I was told in my final follow-up interview that I wasn't really interested in becoming a psychotherapist … it seemed quite, quite unbelievable."

A look of pain passed over Freya Woburn's face. She was abrupt when she replied.

"Yes … the man who interviewed you then—he's been removed from that role."

"But it didn't get taken further, and they didn't come back to me to say that I would be reinterviewed."

"No. Not then. And I do believe that the then group of people responsible was at fault in not doing so. As so often happens in organisations, there was a failure to take appropriate action. And a lot of people, not just you, have suffered as a result. Careers have been blocked for no good reason. The exclusivity of those days, I feel, has organisational roots. To tease out the meaning of it is going to take some time. The important thing now, though, is for us to acknowledge to people like yourself that we didn't behave properly in view of your applications, and to take active steps to put that right." David sat silently. What was she going to say? How could this be taken forward? She sat forward slightly, gazing at him with blue eyes, which, though faded with age, were sharp and intelligent looking.

"Would you be interested in training? Have you still got the financial resources?"

He was startled at this very direct question. He dealt with the question of financial resources first. "I could manage financially," he said. "I was lucky enough to get an inheritance. But would it be a question of being reinterviewed?"

"No. You have already had large numbers of interviews from different people over the years. I have been tasked with finding out from you what you would make of an offer of being accepted on to the training, to start at the next intake of students." She sat back in her chair, looking at the smoky burnt panels of glass on the front of the wood-stove, through which the fire could be seen, burning less brightly now, and she suddenly rose stiffly to her feet and, opening the front of the stove, fed in a small log that she selected from a wicker basket by the fire. She raked around a bit with a small gold-coloured poker that hung by the hearth, and the log began to sputter as it caught fire from the newly-awakened flames. She banged the door shut again with a hefty clang and sat back down in her chair, wiping her hands fastidiously on a tissue. "You were actually well thought of when the Radcliffe looked again at your notes, despite what you were told by your last interviewer."

"I am surprised that the notes have been kept," he said, and she smiled. "Kept more from organisational inertia and over-load than anything else, I would suspect," she said. "But your interviewers generally said reasonably positive things about you, and that's very telling in an atmosphere when reasons are being sought to turn people down."

David considered. He could say that he would like time to think over the offer. That would be reasonable. But, rather impulsive as he was, he wanted the matter settled. The organisational climate might change again with an influx of new people and he wouldn't want to miss this opportunity. Slowly, he raised his eyes from the Persian rug and said, with some hesitation, that he thought that he didn't need time to go away and think it over. He would be glad to accept such an inviting offer. She smiled warmly at him.

"Well, look, we can leave it there then, I can report back to the Radcliffe. We'll write to you with a confirmation, and details of next steps. Is there anything else you'd like to ask?"

"I'm sure that further questions will occur to me in due course," he said, "but at the moment I can't think of anything. Just to say that I am pleased that there has been a change in stance towards applicants."

"We are aware that people have been treated in an inco-herent manner with different interviewers having different views. Applicants being sent away again and again, but invited to reapply, being kept dangling for many years in an inappropriate and cruel way. It's an abuse of power, and I'm also very glad there has been a change in stance. It's been right to make a change for a long time, and I wish it had changed earlier. People's lives, not only their professional lives, have been blighted. Wild comment being made in interviews, husbands and wives being separated, with one accepted and the other not. Things like that haven't helped the reputation of the Radcliffe."

"I agree with you." David sighed, and there was a brief silence. He had the feeling that this silence was a pleasant one, the warmth of the fire, the slight aroma of wood smoke, the agreeable setting, and he realised that he felt this in an emotional sense too. The turbulence of so many unpleasant meetings with Radcliffe interviewers was over now. He could relax, let down his guard a little. "Well, I'm very pleased with the outcome of this meeting," he said. "I'll be glad to train and to function more adequately in my work as a result."

She smiled, didn't say anything more but led him to the door and shook his hand. He wandered in the snowy street, almost without noticing where he was going, and found himself in the park. He decided to celebrate the occasion by having coffee at the café before heading back to work. Underfoot, the fresh snow was deep, and his footsteps began to fill with fresh snow almost immediately. The large flakes falling in front of his eyes created a dreaminess in him, and he enjoyed the contrast between the grey of the bushes and tree trunks around him and the white fluffs of snow floating down and laying themselves on top of their predecessors to add to the increasing depth. He was reminded of days in the hills when he was small, the trees and the snow, the similar silence, and all around him the smell of pine trees. The small birds in the bushes rustled and then were still as he approached, and he saw a blackbird hopping deliberately along at the side of the path, yellow bill and the bright glass bead eyes standing out clearly in the light created by the white snow. He realised that it was singing quietly, as though under its breath, and he paused to listen. The bird angled its head sideways, looking at him as it sang, as though to itself, and David wondered why it was singing like this on a winter's day. It was remarkable, and he walked on feeling that it was a good omen, that spring might not be far off.

He was able to tell Jack and Marie that same evening on the phone. Jack laughed. He told David that it was an opportunity that he wouldn't want to turn down, but did he really have to spend the money, use all that time and go through the ordeal of training? Such hard work. The life of a psychotherapist was not exactly an easy one ... difficult patients, it all being an emotional strain ... and so on. David took all this with a good grace, realising that he was being teased and that actually Jack was pleased for him, and was glad to have him within the Radcliffe orbit.

When he rang Clara she was delighted on his behalf, and suggested going out for a meal to celebrate. It would have to be at the end of the week, she said, as she was finishing writing a paper and evenings were busy. David went to meet her at the restaurant she had selected with a frisson of anxiety but also a comfortable sense that he could be on equal terms with her; he was no longer the Radcliffe reject. He laughed ruefully to himself as he walked down the road; what appalling idealisation that was, of the Radcliffe, the notion he had that being accepted conferred a slightly superhuman status on him. He saw Clara waving from across the road and went over to join her.

"What were you laughing at?" she asked. "I saw you smiling to yourself." She followed this up with a warm embrace. "Congratulations," she said. "You must be pleased that the Radcliffe has changed its tune."

"Yes—that was what I was laughing at," he confessed. "I was just thinking that we could be on equal terms now, both therapists, and I was going on to myself about the idealisation of the Radcliffe—it's so pernicious." She laughed too and agreed with him. She led the way into the restaurant. It wasn't quite what he would have chosen: a Japanese restaurant with a cosy atmosphere and, fortunately for his comfort, western-type tables to sit at. He slid into a seat and Clara sat down opposite him.

"Sake?" he said. "This calls for a celebration."

"Yes—why not? It certainly is something to celebrate." The warmth of the sake removed the last vestiges of chilliness from their walk to the restaurant in the cold, and from their relationship. Clara was describing the *douleur* of writing her paper— appropriately enough it was about loss in the psychoanalytic literature, and here she was coping with the loss of her relationship. She was jokey and upbeat and David wondered if she was putting on a bit of an act for his benefit, wanting perhaps, in addition, to pose as someone who could face the ending of a long-term relationship with some equanimity.

The delicately-flavoured sushi was followed by little mouthfuls of fried octopus. Then some tempura, with the tails of the prawns in their new exoskeleton of light hot batter crisply sticking out of the steaming bowls of soupy noodles. Glancing up, David could see a pottery model of a smiling cat with paw raised. Clara laughed.

"That's the Japanese way of beckoning you in. Or in this case, a cat—they often seem to have that in their restaurants, or even outside, a cat beckoning you in." At that moment the thought struck David that the question was precisely this: was Clara going to welcome a relationship with him? On a sake high he reached across the table past the bowls of tempura and the chopsticks and took her hand in his.

"Well, what's it going to be, Clara?" he asked her, keeping a light note in his voice, a slightly humorous note in case she was going to reject him. "Are you going to invite me in? How did Bob Dylan say it: something about coming in and sheltering from the storm?" He almost half sang, half chanted the last few words, and she laughed.

"I know that song," she said. Then she took his hand in both hers and smiled at him. "You must know the answer, David." She was suddenly all gravity, looking at him with her green eyes. "I'd like nothing better."

"So it's a question of reader, I married him," he said daringly. She laughed again.

"Are you going to be literary as well as cool?" He laughed too, with a sudden sense of relief: a future life with Clara lay ahead.

# ABOUT THE AUTHOR

**R. L. Jannaway** is a psychotherapist and writer.